A PRECIOUS GIFT

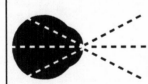

This Large Print Book carries the
Seal of Approval of N.A.V.H.

A PRECIOUS GIFT

SHELLEY SHEPARD GRAY

THORNDIKE PRESS
A part of Gale, a Cengage Company

Copyright © 2019 by Shelley Shepard Gray.
The Walnut Creek Series.
Thorndike Press, a part of Gale, a Cengage Company.

Thorndike Press® Large Print Christian Fiction.
The text of this Large Print edition is unabridged.
Other aspects of the book may vary from the original edition.
Set in 19 pt. Plantin.

LIBRARY OF CONGRESS CIP DATA ON FILE.
CATALOGUING IN PUBLICATION FOR THIS BOOK
IS AVAILABLE FROM THE LIBRARY OF CONGRESS

ISBN-13: 978-1-4328-7267-0 (hardcover alk. paper)

Published in 2020 by arrangement with Gallery Books, an imprint of Simon & Schuster, Inc.

Printed in Mexico
1 2 3 4 5 6 7 24 23 22 21 20

*For Lynne, who agreed
with me that Kyle and Gabby
had a story that needed
to be told.*

Children are a gift from the Lord,
they are a reward from Him.

— Psalm 127:3

When God sends us a stony
path, He provides us with
strong shoes.

— Proverb

ONE

It was always difficult to meet new people, especially friends of friends of the woman he intended to marry one day. So, when one of them asked Kyle Lambright about himself, he reckoned the best way to do that was to share a story about him and his brother. Leaning forward in his chair, he began.

"You see, from the time I was four or five, my favorite thing to do was follow my big brother Harley around."

With a feeling of dread, Gabby sat down on the side of the bathtub and reluctantly picked up the plastic stick she'd just dropped on the linoleum floor. Her heart was pounding and her hand was shaking. And her eyes? Well, her vision was already blurred from the tears she was fighting back.

But no matter how much her body was attempting to ignore the information right in front of her eyes, she knew it was no use.

No matter how much the rest of her body wanted to reject the clear blue digital line on the plastic stick in her hand, it wasn't about to go away.

No, the truth was right there in front of her eyes, clear as day. She was pregnant.

She braced a hand against the cold tile and attempted to take another breath. What was she going to do? How was she going to tell Kyle? Or her friends? Or Kyle's parents? Or her mother?

Her stomach clenched. How was she ever going to tell her mother? Just thinking about her mother's reaction made her feel nauseated.

"Gabby?" The door shook with her mother's impatient raps. "Gabrielle, are you in there still?"

Still staring at that stick, she nodded. Then forced herself to speak. "Yes."

The door handle jiggled. "The door's locked."

She was eighteen years old and in the bathroom. Of course it was locked. "I know."

"Well, unlock it and come on out."

Gabby's eyes darted to the open pregnancy test kit on the floor. To her phone on the counter. To the can of Sprite that she'd picked up because it was the only thing that sounded remotely appealing. Each looked like evidence of her pregnancy. Each was sure to be an unwanted sign that would only ask for trouble in this house.

"Gabby?"

"Hold on, Mom. I'll be out in five."

She could practically see her mother tapping her shoe in irritation. "I don't have five minutes to wait for you. I have to get to work in twenty minutes." She jiggled the handle again. "Come on out. What are you doing in there anyway?"

"Uh, going to the bathroom?"

"For all this time?" Worry entered her tone. "How come? Are you sick?"

"No."

"Well, then come on. I'm sure your hair looks fine."

Getting to her feet, Gabby scrambled around the small space, stuffing the test, the box it came in, and her phone in her purse, then zipped it shut for good measure. Then she washed her hands yet again before pulling open the door.

"Sorry."

As she expected, her mother was still standing in the doorway, looking irritated and stressed. "Honestly, you would think by now you would be more respectful of other people in this house." She rushed by Gabby and slammed the door in her face. "We have one bathroom for you, me, and your brother, Lane. Plus you know, *you know* that I always go to work at eleven on Saturdays."

"I said I was sorry." Gabby rolled her eyes and forced herself to stay in the hallway even though it was incredibly tempting to simply walk away.

She heard the toilet flush and the sink turn on. "Don't forget that Lane needs to be picked up from wrestling practice at five."

"I haven't forgotten." And honestly, Lane was almost seventeen. He'd have no problem reminding Gabby himself — or catching a ride with a friend if she wasn't around.

"I left you a grocery list on the counter and fifty dollars. Don't forget to go to the store."

"I won't." Hadn't she done the majority of the grocery shopping and cooking for the last two years?

"I'm going out after work, too. Will you two be all right?"

Gabby knew this was a rhetorical question. An answer wasn't expected. Well, not an honest one, anyway. "Lane and I will be fine, Mom."

The door opened. Her mother had on another thick layer of mascara and a fresh coat of pink lipstick. As usual, she looked pretty and put together. Far younger than forty years old.

"So, what are you going to do today?" her mother asked, sounding much more like herself. "Do you have plans?"

Before she picked up Lane, went to the store, and cooked dinner, she had something she had to do. "I'm going to see Kyle."

The muscles around her mother's mouth tightened before she nodded. Which was kind of a step forward. Mom didn't like her boyfriend, not because of who he was — a nice boy nine months older than Gabby — but because he was Amish. Her mother had a real problem with anyone who was Amish. However, from practically the moment Gabby had first met Kyle, she'd felt drawn to him. Their differences had never mattered to her. Only the fact that she liked him so very much.

"I don't want the two of you hanging out here by yourselves," her mother said. For about the hundredth time.

"We won't be," Gabby replied, telling her mother the same thing she always said. Though, she realized with a flutter of nerves, it was also too late for that warning now.

"What will you do?"

"I'm not sure."

Her mother opened her mouth, then shut it quickly. No doubt Mom was already mentally preparing her latest speech that highlighted all kinds of warnings about the dangers of teenage hormones and the harm they could do to the best laid plans.

It was a conversation they'd had many, many times. And one Gabby really, really didn't want to talk about, since well, it was now evident that her mother had been right.

"Mom, don't you have to go to work?"

"What?" She glanced at her watch

then winced. "Oh my gosh. Erin's going to kill me if I walk in late again. Bye."

"Bye," Gabby whispered as she watched her mother hurry down their narrow hallway, pick up an oversize tote from the kitchen counter, and rush out the front door.

Leaning against the wall, another fresh bout of tears threatened to fall.

What in the world was she going to do? She was eighteen, a product of a single mom, practically responsible for her younger brother, and was now pregnant because she and her boyfriend had taken things too far.

It was everything her mother had

warned her could happen.

It was also everything she'd promised her mother never would.

TWO

"My brother Harley had a large group of best friends, which everyone called the Eight. They'd first met when they were really young and had remained close for over a decade. It never seemed to matter to any of them that some were English, some were Mennonite, and some were Amish like us."

"Careful now, Kyle," Jimmy called out. "That bag of feed is heavy."

"I got it." Picking up the forty-pound bag, Kyle hoisted it on his shoulder to carry it into the barn. It was times like these when he felt he deserved a medal for biting his tongue. He was almost nineteen and strong as an ox. He'd also been working next to his two older brothers and father all his life. That meant he'd carried his fair share of feed bags, and then some.

But no matter how many times he did a man's work, one of those three men felt the need to call out a warning like he was still a boy. He'd learned to simply do his part without making a fuss. Keeping the bag solidly balanced on one shoulder, Kyle strode into the barn.

The inside was at least twenty degrees warmer than the frosty temperature outside. Added to the welcome warmth was a hint of moisture from the filled water troughs in each stall. The change in climate felt good.

But what really lifted his spirits were the four heads that poked out from each stall. Four beautiful, sturdy horses with alert eyes, long eyelashes, and powdery soft noses. "Hiya, girls."

Lightning whickered a hello.

After tossing the bag on the top of the pile, he walked over to her, casually brushing a hand along the mare's forelock as he did so. All four of the horses were beauties and good workers, but Lightning owned his heart.

"How's my girl?" He rubbed her

brown neck, liking how her thick winter coat felt in between his fingers. When she pawed at the ground and leaned her head closer, he chuckled. "I know. You're ready to go for a run, but you won't be thinking that thirty minutes in. It's cold out. Mighty cold."

Lightning blew out a whiff of air, making Kyle imagine she was annoyed with him. He laughed as he gave her one last affectionate pat before heading back outside.

Jimmy was standing by the pile of feed and glaring at him. "What took you so long?"

"I wasn't long, brother."

His eyes narrowed. "Were you playing with those horses again?"

This time he didn't bother to hide

his exasperation. "All I was doing was telling Lightning hello. I wasn't playing."

"You treat those workhorses like pets."

"*Nee,* I treat them like horses, Jimmy." Wondering what was going on with his usually even-keeled brother, he said, "You're awfully grumpy. What's gotten into you?"

"Nothing. I'm fine."

Jimmy's words sounded like machine-gun fire, they were so harsh and clipped. Kyle raised his eyebrows. "You sure about that?"

"*Jah,*" Jimmy bit out before shaking his head. "Sorry. I know I don't sound like myself. I just have a need to get these chores done so I can go see Sarah."

His brother and Sarah had been a couple for years and had been engaged for more than a year. Everyone in the family thought they would have been married by now, but they still hadn't set a date, which nobody else seemed to understand. In contrast, Harley and Katie had gone from mere friends to husband and wife in less than ten months.

"Is everything okay with Sarah?" Kyle asked tentatively.

Suddenly looking exhausted, Jimmy shrugged. "I don't know. Lately, everything I do seems to annoy her. I think she's frustrated with me."

He was dying to ask what, exactly, Sarah was frustrated about, but he didn't want to pry too much. After all, this was more than Jimmy usually confided.

He decided to say something safe. "That doesn't sound like her."

"It isn't." After another pause, Jimmy added, "We're getting a lot of questions about why we haven't gotten married yet. It's starting to chafe both of our nerves. But that ain't my fault, you know?"

Kyle was taken aback by his brother's statement. "I'm surprised that's bothering you. You've never worried about other people's opinions."

"You're right. I never have. But Sarah ain't cut from the same cloth. She worries about everyone and everything." Lowering his voice, he said, "I noticed her glaring at Katie at church the other day. I think she feels that Harley and she should've waited for us to marry."

Worrying about such a thing seemed like a waste of time. "Mamm and Daed wouldn't have cared if you and Harley had gotten married on the same day."

"I know that, but deep down, I think Sarah believes I'm the reason we haven't married yet."

Kyle was stunned. Sarah's mother had been diagnosed with cancer a year ago. He'd assumed the delay had something to do with that. "Is she right?"

"Kind of." Looking pained, he said, "Kyle, I'm just not sure she's the one."

"Wow." Jimmy and Sarah had seemed like a perfect match. Both were Amish, both came from families who were close-knit and prosperous. They also had the same temperament and wanted the same things in life.

Sarah also had the benefit of having their father's approval, which wasn't an easy thing to achieve. In short, the pair was everything that he and Gabby were not.

Still stepping carefully, he said, "I don't know what to say."

"That's because there ain't nothing for you to say," Jimmy said lightly. "I mean, it ain't like you have any experience in love."

Kyle's temper flared. Here he was, weighing each word carefully, and Jimmy was talking down to him. Again. "You know I have a girlfriend."

"Gabby ain't a real girlfriend, Kyle."

He could feel his face heating up. Gabby and he had been as close as a couple could get. He loved her. And while he wasn't exactly proud of himself for getting carried away with her two months ago, he didn't regret what had happened. She was everything to him.

But because of her mother's disdain for the Amish and his parents' insistence that being married to someone of their "own kind" was the best way to go, they'd hid just how serious things had gotten.

"She is to me."

"But —"

"It's true, Jimmy. Both Gabby and I take our relationship seriously."

"All right . . . but let me ask you this. Where can this relationship with her actually go?"

"Go?"

"*Jah.* I mean, it ain't like you two can have a future together."

Though Gabby was English and he was Amish, he'd thought of nothing but having a future with her. He'd even realized that he would have to jump the fence to make that happen. "We might."

Jimmy smirked. "Yeah, right. Like she would become Amish."

"That's not the only option, Jimmy."

"Come on." Jimmy smiled. However, it slowly vanished as it became apparent that he realized Kyle wasn't joking around. Not even a little bit. Sounding a lot more serious, he said, "Kyle, you need to get your head out of the clouds and think about what you're saying."

"My head ain't in the clouds." His feet were firmly on the ground. So much so, that he had even entertained the thought of talking with their parents about his options. That conversation wouldn't be easy, but he was starting to realize that nothing worth having was.

"All right then, how about you stop thinking about Gabby's charms?"

Her charms? Barely holding his

temper in check, Kyle said, "I think you'd better stop. Don't speak about Gabby like that."

"Like what? That she's gorgeous and has a body —"

"Don't."

"I'm not trying to be disrespectful —"

"But you are." Kyle was seething. He could only imagine how Jimmy would react if he said anything like that about Sarah. "You need to shut up."

"*Nee,* it's you who is needing to grow up."

"I'm man enough to haul feed bags and do my part on this farm."

"You know that don't mean a thing. You have responsibilities to the family."

Responsibilities that he'd never shirked. Afraid to say something he would later regret, Kyle bit his lip. Hefting another bag of feed onto his shoulder, he turned toward the barn.

"Hey, don't run away! We should talk —"

"Nee."

"Kyle!"

"What is going on?" Harley called out from his bicycle as he rode up the drive. "Jimmy, I could hear you the moment I pulled off the road."

"You're going to have to ask our little brother about that," Jimmy said.

"Kyle?" Harley prodded.

Great. Now he was going to have to defend himself and his relationship to *two* brothers. "Don't worry about it," he said as he quickly grabbed another bag of feed and started walking.

Behind him, he could hear Harley murmur something to Jimmy, then pick up a bag and follow him.

"You okay?"

"Oh, I'm great. *Wunderbaar,*" he added sarcastically.

Harley tossed the bag on the pile so easily, it might as well have been a bag of feathers. "Jimmy said you two were talking about Gabby."

Looking out the open door of the barn, Kyle could see Jimmy standing there, watching the two of them. "We were, though the whole conversation started because of Sarah."

"Really?"

Kyle grunted.

Harley winced. "Ah. Let me guess, Jimmy had some opinions about your girlfriend?"

"He did, which he wasn't afraid to share."

They started walking back to the entrance. When the three of them were facing each other, Harley blew out a sigh. "Do I even want to wade into this discussion?"

"Nee."

"It might help ya if Harley wades in," Jimmy blurted.

"It will not," Kyle replied. "And I'm telling you right now that I might be younger than the two of you, but I'm also a grown man. You need to respect me *and* my girlfriend."

Harley's eyebrows rose. "Jimmy, what did you say to him?"

Just as Jimmy opened his mouth, Kyle bit out, "Don't. Don't you dare say it again."

"Whoa," Harley murmured. "Okay, I think all of us need to calm down."

Jimmy crossed his arms over his chest. "I know you're *gut* at helping everyone in this family, Harley, but our brother here is about to make a big mistake. Someone has to speak plainly to him."

"*Nee,* you need to respect my judgment!" Kyle said.

"But —"

"I agree with Kyle," Harley interjected quickly. "Jimmy, you and I know that Kyle already has a father. He don't need us telling him what to do, too."

And just like that, Jimmy's stance eased. "You're right. Kyle, I am sorry if I overstepped myself. I . . . I should've kept my mouth shut."

Jimmy was right. He should have. But seeing Harley's expression, Kyle knew that saying such a thing would only make their oldest brother irritated. And no one ever wanted Harley upset with them. Everyone in the family depended on Harley in one way or another. He was the sibling who was the most responsible. The sibling who always smoothed the way with their sometimes demanding parents. He was also the sibling who Kyle had always wanted to make proud.

"It's all right," he said at last. "Don't worry about it none, Jimmy."

"*Danke,*" Jimmy murmured.

Harley looked from Kyle to Jimmy to Kyle again. "Now, should we talk about things?"

"I'd rather not," Kyle said. He just wanted to end the conversation as quickly as possible.

"All right then." Looking just beyond Kyle, Harley smiled slightly. "Hmm. I'm thinking now is probably a bad time, anyway."

"And why is that?" Jimmy asked.

"Because it looks like Kyle here has some company."

Kyle and Jimmy turned to where Harley was looking, and Kyle felt his whole body tense up.

Gabby, dressed in jeans, boots, and a ruby-red sweater, was walking up their driveway. Her long dark hair was in a ponytail, sunglasses covered her brown eyes, and the only thing in her hand was a small purse. Kyle could hardly take his eyes off her.

The warmth that ran through him every time he caught sight of her came back full force . . . until he realized that she looked tense and upset.

"Something's wrong," he told his brothers before walking out to her.

One of them said something, but he had no idea what.

All he cared about was seeing her

again . . . and trying to make things better.

THREE

"Sometimes I would trail after them, sure that they wouldn't notice I was there. I wanted to be just like my big brother, and I was fascinated by all of Harley's non-Amish friends."

All the best-case scenarios that Gabby had been trying to convince herself might actually happen plummeted with each step closer to Kyle. There was no way this visit was going to end on a positive note. No, it was going to be really bad.

Both of Kyle's older brothers were home, and both of them were watching her so intently, she felt like she was trespassing.

When they discovered her reason for coming over, there was no telling what they were going to do — or say. Well, except that it was going to be bad.

And Kyle! She knew how close he was to his siblings and how much he idolized his older brothers. There was a very good chance that he was going to put all the blame on her shoulders and turn away from her. After all, it had happened before. From what her mother had said, it had happened exactly like that with her. Her mom had been in love with an Amish boy and had foolishly believed that everything between them was going to work out in spite of all the odds piled against them. Instead, he'd abandoned her completely.

Her mother had been forced to go through her pregnancy by herself, with only the minimum of support from her family. Gabby's father had pulled so far away, into the depths of his Amish community, that there had been no way for her mother to get any financial assistance at all.

She hadn't even been able to let Gabby's father know about her birth.

Thinking about that, and how the whole experience had made her mother lose almost all trust in men,

Gabby's heart sank. This was going to happen again; she was going to repeat history.

"Gabby, hiya!" Kyle called out as he walked toward her. "This is a mighty *gut* surprise."

In spite of all the worries churning inside her, she smiled. This was one of the things she liked about him. He was such a warm and friendly type of guy. "Hiya, back," she teased. He always made her feel special and worthy.

He laughed. "Are you making fun of me again?"

"Never." When he stepped closer to her side, her body reacted. She felt her spirits lift and her tense muscles relax. No matter what happened in their future, she was so glad she'd come right over to see him.

Leaning down, he murmured, "Wouldja like me to teach you some Pennsylvania Dutch?"

She tried to ignore the familiar buzzing sensation she always felt around him and played along. "I could be wrong, but I don't think 'hiya' is in another language," she teased.

"Maybe not." He reached for her hand and squeezed it gently. "What brings you over? I'm not complaining, but seeing you here in the morning is a surprise."

This was it. She'd kind of hoped to have at least a few more minutes before she told him the news and lost him forever.

She cleared her throat. "There's something I need to talk to you about."

His lighthearted expression faded. "It sounds serious."

"It is. It's really serious," she said. She glanced at his brothers again. They were still standing in the center of the driveway and watching them. "Um, is now a bad time?"

Kyle glanced toward his brothers, muttered something under his breath, and then turned back to her. "Now's fine. I was just helping Jimmy carry some bags of feed into the barn. I finished."

"Oh." Every once in a while, she would forget just how different his life was from hers. This was one of those times. He worked by his brothers' sides, doing all sorts of chores that she'd never thought about. "Are you sure you can get away?"

"Of course." He tugged on her hand. "Come on. Let's go say hi, and then we'll go somewhere to talk."

"All right."

As Kyle led her to them, she felt awkward, which was stupid. She'd been over to Kyle's house at least a dozen times, and no one ever made a big deal about how she wasn't Amish or looked different, they simply accepted her as she was. And though she made sure she didn't wear anything revealing or too tight, she never tried to dress in anything other than her usual.

She wouldn't have worn anything too revealing to any boy's house.

Every time she'd come over, his parents had been nice and his siblings had been friendly. His sister Betty could have been a friend she would've made on her own, they got along so well. So she knew she shouldn't have been worried about talking to Harley and Jimmy at all.

But, of course, she'd never come over for a reason like this. Who knew how everyone would react to her from here on out? They might soon want nothing to do with her.

At last — and all too soon — they stopped in front of his brothers. "Jimmy, Harley, as you can see, Gabby has stopped by."

She waved a hand. "Hi."

Right away, Harley smiled. "*Gut matin,* Gabby. How are you?"

"Good morning. Um, I'm okay," she replied, hating that her voice was shaky. "What about you?"

Some of the humor in his eyes faded as he looked at her with more concern. "Me? I'm *gut,* though I *canna* speak for Jimmy."

Boy, she needed to keep it together! Hoping to sound a lot more normal, she smiled. "Jimmy, I hope you are good, too."

"I am well enough," he said.

"That is good," she replied, feeling like every word they were saying sounded more stilted than the last. Boy, this was awkward.

Jimmy stepped toward the house. Looking pensive, he said, "Kyle, do you want me to fetch Mamm and tell her Gabby is here?"

"*Nee.* Gabby and I are going to go over to the picnic table and talk."

"It's cold out," Harley warned.

"We'll be fine."

Jimmy frowned and pointedly stared at their entwined hands. "But, don'tcha think that Mamm —"

Beside her, Kyle inhaled. It was obvious that his patience with Jimmy was nearing an end. "For the —"

"We'll see you later, Gabby," Harley interrupted. "James and I've got a lot to do in the barn." He smiled slightly at Kyle before ushering his brother away.

Kyle winked at Gabby. "Come on, then. Let's go talk."

When they got to the picnic table, which was sanded smooth and painted a dark forest green, Gabby climbed on the top and sat down.

Kyle clambered up beside her and rested his hands behind him, leaning back. Just like he was at the beach or something, he tilted his face toward the sun and closed his eyes. "I love clear, sunny days like this in December, don't you?"

"It's all right." She was so nervous, it could be pouring rain and she'd hardly notice.

He opened one eye. "It's all right? Come now, Gabby. The sun's out, and the scent of pine is in the air. Christmas is just around the corner. It's a perfect time of year."

"I could have sworn that you said the same thing about spring, though you mentioned baby animals, buds on trees, and egg salad sandwiches."

His lips twitched. "I have always liked a good egg salad."

"Oh, you. You're incorrigible."

"Maybe I'm simply happy to be spending time with you, Gabby. You make me happy."

Her heart melted a little. Even though she knew she should be doing the exact opposite — to be preparing herself for him to reject her, or for them to fight, or to blame her for everything — her foolish heart was still beating just for him.

No wonder she was in the situation she was in! She seemed to have no sense of self-preservation around him.

"What about you?"

"Me?"

"*Jah.* Do I make you happy?"

He did. In fact, he made everything in her world better.

But that wasn't why she was here.

When she didn't say anything, a line formed between Kyle's eyebrows. "Gabby, did you come over here to break up with me?"

"What? No!" This was getting worse and worse.

Kyle stood up and walked a few steps away. "Then what's wrong?" he asked, turning back to her. "Have I done something to upset you?" His voice was pensive. Hoarse. "If I did, all ya have to do is tell me."

"Kyle, you didn't do anything —"

"*Nee,* listen. Gabby, I promise, once I know what the problem is, I can fix it." He smiled tightly. "I promise that I can make it better."

Not this problem! "Kyle, you didn't do anything wrong. I'm not mad at you. You do make me happy."

"You sure?"

"I'm sure. Positive."

"Okay, but I have to tell ya that I'm having a hard time believing you, on account of you don't look all that happy right now. Matter of fact, you look kind of green, if you want to know the truth."

If she did look green it was because she was starting to feel pretty sick. "That's because what I came over to tell you is really hard to say."

"Well, worrying about what you're gonna say is just about to kill me. Just say it."

"I'm pregnant."

He opened his mouth, obviously prepared to comfort her with a few sweet phrases, then froze as it became obvious that her words had just sunk in.

And . . . things had just gone from bad to worse.

FOUR

"But, of course, Harley would always send me back home, saying that I was too young to keep up."

Kyle looked like someone had run him over with a bus. "Gabby, did I hear ya right? You . . . you're with child?"

Swallowing hard, she nodded. Then, just to make sure there was no misunderstanding, she whispered, "I'm pregnant with your baby. I mean, our baby." Hating that each word was tumbling out of her mouth in a jumble of stops and starts, Gabby took a deep breath and tried again. "I mean, it, no . . . I mean, *the baby* is yours."

His confused expression melted into something sweet as he pulled her into his arms. "I know that," he said softly as he ran a hand down her hair. "Come now, don't you think I remember every detail of what happened that night?"

She did, too. Her dark car. The "just one more kiss" that had turned into so much more. The fumbling. The embarrassed chuckles and the kisses. Neither of them had known what they were doing, but it hadn't seemed to matter. All she'd been aware of was how much in love with him she was.

Looking back at him, she blushed, though she noticed that he wasn't blushing at all. Instead, he was watching her intently. Waiting for her to speak again.

"I remember everything, too," she said at last.

His expression warmed as he rubbed her shoulder blades. "Now, when did you find out?"

His calm manner helped ease her nerves. Scooting a few inches away, she focused on what she knew. "This morning. My body was acting strange and I started feeling a little weird."

"Weird? How so?"

"Um, I felt nauseated. Tired."

"Ah."

Remembering how sick to her stomach she'd felt for most of the last week, she continued. "Anyway, when I realized that I didn't have the flu, I started wondering if something else might have been going on. So, um, I drove all the way to New Philly and bought a test at a Walgreens there last night."

Looking at her intently, he said, "Did you go by yourself?"

"Well, yeah. I had to wait for my mom to come home from work. Then I made up a story about how a girlfriend of mine wanted to borrow a pair of shoes." Her mother hadn't questioned her story one bit. She'd barely remembered to grab a pair of heels before darting to the car.

"And then you took the test this morning?"

She nodded. "The directions say that you're supposed to do the test as soon as you get up." Hearing her stilted explanation, she mentally rolled her eyes. How can she be having Kyle's baby but be embarrassed to talk about peeing on a stick?

Sitting on the picnic table, Kyle was still looking at her quietly. "What did you do when you got the results?"

"What do you mean?"

"I mean, did you tell your mother?" He folded his hands around the edge of the table. "I guess you can tell that I hate you were by yourself."

She was pretty much gaping at Kyle. Never had she imagined that he would be thinking of something like that. No, she'd thought he would be more panicked and mad.

Returning back to his question, she shook her head. "Of course I didn't tell my mom. There was no way."

"But, Gabby . . ."

"Kyle, she would have freaked out. You know what she's like."

He still looked confused. "What about Lane?"

"Kyle, all I did was hide the box and try to get the nerve to come over here to tell you." No way was she ready to share how her mother had been jiggling the doorknob.

"What did you think was going to

happen when you told me?"

"I was afraid —" She stopped abruptly, not wanting him to know just how worried she'd been about his reaction. When he continued to stare at her, she simply shrugged. "I, well, I don't know."

His blue eyes flared before he carefully tamped down his worry. "Oh, Gabby. Come here." He pulled her back into his arms. But this time, it wasn't just a loose, careful hug.

No, it was an embrace. His arms were wrapped securely around her, and his lips were resting on her forehead. It was almost like he was doing everything he possibly could do to offer her comfort and support.

She rested against him, breathing in his strength. Here they were, sitting on a picnic table in the middle of his lawn. His brothers were nearby. No doubt his mother and at least one of his sisters were watching from the window. Every other time they'd been together at his house, they'd hardly touched.

Surely his entire family was shocked.

But Kyle didn't seem to care who saw them.

"It's gonna be okay, Gabby," he murmured as he shifted and eased her closer to his body. She shifted until she was practically sitting on his lap. His arms, so strong, wrapped around her securely. Though she wasn't an especially small girl, she felt small in his arms.

Little by little, she relaxed against him, resting her face in his neck, looping her arms around his neck. He was warm and smelled like the grass he liked so much, and faintly of horses, and like Kyle.

He smelled comforting and re-assuring. There was no telling what would happen next, or what even tomorrow would bring. But all that seemed to matter was that she wasn't alone and that he wasn't yelling at her or making her feel ashamed.

She closed her eyes and rested against him.

One hand ran down her spine. She felt the weight of it, and how careful he was being with her. Like she was fragile.

No, like she mattered.

"There, that's better. Let's sit here for a moment, okay? I want to hold you, *jah*?"

His words were so sweet. So different from how she'd feared he would react. So much the opposite of how her mother said she'd been treated. She was at a loss for words.

So, instead of saying a thing, she relaxed against Kyle and let herself find comfort in his arms. She hadn't known it, but she'd needed this. The reassurance. The tenderness. Tears pricked her eyes again.

Stupid tears.

She hadn't come over to cry on his shoulder, but it looked like that was happening again. She inhaled, hoping to stave off the worst of it.

He patted her shoulder blade. "Gabby, are ya crying?"

"No."

He pulled away, looked down at her face. Swiped her cheek with a finger. "Are you sure about that?" he teased.

"I don't want to cry right now. I'm trying not to."

"Maybe you can't help it."

Maybe she couldn't. Honestly, her whole body was acting strange. Stupid hormones, too. "I'm better." But then, of course, one rebel tear slid down her cheek.

"Hmm. Looks like you need something else to think about."

"Like what?" She was eighteen and pregnant.

"Like this," he murmured, just before he kissed her.

His kiss affected her like it always did. It pushed all reason and caution away and only made her think of him. Before she was really aware of what she was doing, Gabby had her hands around his neck and was kissing him back wholeheartedly.

"Mmm-hmm," he murmured, holding her closer.

"Kyle Lambright! What in the world are you doing on our picnic table?"

Oh! That was his mother. Gabby jerked away from Kyle and pressed her hands to her face.

She felt Kyle turn toward his front door. "I'm kissing Gabby, Mamm!" he said.

"Kyle, don't be cheeky. I want to know why."

He paused. "All right, then. Gabby and I need to come inside and talk to you."

"Now?"

"*Jah.* It's important, Mamm."

"Come on, then. I'll make us some tea."

The moment Mrs. Lambright closed the door, Gabby glared at him. "What are we going inside to talk to your mother about?"

He grabbed her hand. "About the baby, of course."

Gabby gaped at him. "I didn't come over here to make an announcement, Kyle!" she practically hissed. "I came over to tell you the news."

"I know. And you did tell me."

"So I think we should wait."

"*Nee,* I don't think so," he said as he scooted off the table and gently pulled her off, too. "This is inevitable. We might as well get it over with."

"But . . . I don't want to tell them until I make some decisions. I don't even know what I'm going to do."

He froze in midstep. For the first time since she'd known him, Kyle's expression hardened. "This ain't about just you, Gabby. It's about me, too. *Nee,* it's about the *three* of us."

She was having trouble keeping up. "Three?"

"*Jah.* You, me, and our baby. You aren't alone, Gabby. Not anymore."

Looking determined, he added, "For the rest of our lives, it's now the three of us. We're a family, ain't so?"

They were a family? While those words were sinking in, she followed him into his house.

Kyle hadn't gotten mad. He hadn't walked away.

Neither had he yelled at her or tried to shift the blame to rest firmly on her shoulders. Instead, he was already thinking of them as a unit and was anxious to share the news about the baby with his parents.

So far, nothing that had happened had been anything like she'd imagined.

Not a bit of it.

FIVE

"Usually, I would go back home and wait for Harley to come home. But one day, when I was seven and Harley was thirteen, I only pretended to leave."

For the first time in his life, Kyle felt like thanking his brother Harley for being so closed-mouthed. Harley was a master of hiding his emotions — a direct result from bearing the majority of their stern father's wishes.

Harley's ability to conceal his

72

thoughts had always irritated Kyle. It had made his oldest brother seem far too stern and difficult. It had always made him feel on edge — he'd never known where he'd stood with Harley.

Recently though, Harley had begun to soften a bit. Kyle knew it was because of the recent changes that had occurred between him and Katie. Katie had encouraged him to show and share more of his emotions. And because of her influence and Harley's willingness to do most anything to make her happy, everyone in the Lambright family had benefitted from the softer side of Harley.

But now, as he mentally prepared himself to shock his mother, Kyle was glad that he could mimic his brother's original trait and look completely calm. Gabby needed that.

Though he was no expert on relationships, he knew that she needed him to be at ease and at least appear confident. She didn't need to know that he was currently shaking in his boots.

"Mamm?" he called out when he didn't see her in their pale-yellow kitchen.

"I'm in the living room, Kyle," she replied. "Both Daed and I are."

"We're going to talk to your father right now, too?" Gabby whispered.

"I guess so." He shrugged, hoping he looked far more relaxed than he felt. Keeping his voice low, he added, "I thought he was at a meeting in town."

"Maybe that would have been better."

When he felt her tremble, Kyle squeezed her hand lightly. "This is a good thing. Now you won't have to worry about what he's going to say. We'll get it all over with at one time."

"You're not worried about what they're going to say?"

He shook his head, hoping she believed his lie. Because for sure, he was really worried.

No matter how much he would like it to be different, he knew that the upcoming conversation was not going to go well. His parents didn't like surprises, and they didn't like their children to ignore all of their teachings.

This pregnancy fell into both of those categories.

Their house was big and sprawling, but that didn't mean there was a lot of space in between rooms. Fifteen steps later, he was bringing Gabby into their living room and facing his parents, who were sitting in a pair of cream-colored wing chairs.

After looking pointedly at him and their linked hands, they stared at Gabby.

By his side, Gabby stiffened, then her cheeks slowly turned red. His hands turned clammy.

"It will be all right," he whispered. Though, truth be told, he wasn't sure if he was trying to reassure her or himself.

"Gabby," Daed said at last. "Hello."

"Hi, Mr. Lambright. Mrs. Lambright." Her voice sounded strained.

"Come on, let's sit down," he said. Though he hated to break their connection, Kyle let go of Gabby's hand and gestured to the sofa.

She perched on the edge of the couch. He took a seat right next to her.

When he saw his mother inhale, obviously ready to launch into a speech about how they should not be kissing on the picnic table, Kyle knew he had no choice but to speak fast. Having them embarrass Gabby was not going to make their news any easier to share.

"Mamm, Daed, Gabby came over this morning to tell me some news."

His parents exchanged a concerned look before his mother spoke. "What is it?"

Feeling like Gabby was practically shrinking into the fabric of the couch with every second, Kyle weighed various approaches. Was one way better than another? He wasn't sure.

"Kyle?" Daed prodded.

"Um, there ain't no way to tell you this easily." He glanced at Gabby. She now had her hands folded across her midsection.

"I think you'd best spit out whatever you have to say, son," Daed murmured. "The sooner the better."

"All right then. Gabby is pregnant."

Right there in front of them, his father's face turned to stone. His mother? Well, she looked like she was about to faint.

Visibly attempting to not burst into tears, Gabby hung her head.

He hated that.

Wrapping an arm around her shoulders, he leaned close and whispered, "It's going to be okay," he said again. "No matter what, you aren't alone."

When she met his gaze and nodded, Kyle felt like he'd finally done something right. After one more encouraging nod, he dropped his arm and stared back at his parents. "I know you're surprised. I'm sorry."

His mother now was looking at them with a softer expression. And his father? Well, his expression had gone from stone to something a little less scary.

"How long have you known about this, son?" he asked.

"I just found out today."

"I came over to tell him," Gabby said.

"I see."

"And . . . have you known long?" his *mamm* asked.

"No. I just took the pregnancy test this morning."

"What did your mother say?"

"I haven't told her yet." Her voice quivered. "I wanted to talk to Kyle first."

His mother closed her eyes. "I see." When she opened her eyes again, she stared hard at him. "Kyle, I have no words."

She might say that, but he knew she'd have lots to say the moment Gabby left. "Don't start, Mamm. No one is to blame."

His mother shook her head. "Of course someone is to blame, and that someone is you."

"Mother."

"Don't you act so surprised, son. You know better."

Well aware that Gabby didn't need to hear his mother's upcoming lecture, Kyle lowered his voice. "Mamm, I know it's a shock, but I think we're all shocked right now. Have a care, if you please."

"I'm sorry," Gabby said quietly.

"Nee," his father blurted. "Don't apologize. Not now, anyway."

Whether it was his father's stern expression or his tone, Gabby flinched.

Again, Kyle tried to run interference. "Hey now, he didn't mean —"

"I can speak for myself, son," his father interrupted. Turning to Gabby, his voice softened. "What I am saying is that what's done is done. Ain't so?"

"Yes?"

His mother chuckled. "I'm sure

we'll be having many more talks, but I think if there is one thing that we can all agree on it's that a baby is a blessing. Always."

Kyle felt the rock that had embedded itself in his chest shift. He was going to be able to breathe easier. "Mamm, Daed, even though I know you aren't happy with me, I'm glad we told you."

"*Jah.* Well, we'll be talking to you later, but that is for another time," Mamm said. "Now, Gabby, how are you feeling?"

"Scared. I didn't plan for this to happen. I'm embarrassed, too. I should've known better."

"I meant physically, dear. How are you feeling?"

"Oh! A little achy and a little bit

nauseated."

"You're feeling all that right now?" Kyle asked.

If she hadn't been so nervous, she would have laughed. "Yeah. But I'm okay. I think I'm supposed to feel like this."

He hadn't even thought about things like that. "Oh."

His father gave him a disappointed look.

Gabby cleared her throat and spoke to his mom again. "I read on the Internet that I'm supposed to feel different, right?"

His mother smiled softly. "Yes. The body does a great many things to get ready for this journey." Standing up, she reached out a hand to Gabby. "How about you and I go into the kitchen and see if eating something might help make you feel better?"

She looked at Kyle warily. He nodded. "It's okay. I think that's a *gut* idea. I'll um, sit in here with my *daed* for a little bit."

Gabby's expression relaxed as she followed his mother down the hall.

When the women were out of earshot, Kyle looked his father in the eye. "I know you are disappointed in me."

"I am. You are too young, Kyle."

"You're right."

"And this Gabby — last I heard, her mother didn't even like the two of you seeing each other." He lowered his voice. "I mean, she liked it even less than we did."

"She doesn't." He straightened his shoulders. "But I really do love Gabby, Father. I'm serious about her."

"I hope so, because you two are going to have a long road ahead of you."

"What am I supposed to do, Daed?" he asked. "Should we get married right away? But if we did that, I don't know what we'd do then. I don't have a job. Where are we going to live?" A dozen more questions ran through his head, each one seeming more impossible than the last.

"The first thing you need to do is be by her side, which you did, *jah*?"

Warily, Kyle nodded.

"And then you need to speak to

us and not keep secrets."

He'd done that, too. *"Jah."*

"So, I'm guessing that the next thing to do is visit with Gabby's mother."

He already had a good idea of how it was going to go. "She's going to be so mad. She's going to hate me."

His father scratched his brow. "I could be wrong, but so far it don't sound like Gabby is blaming you. She's blaming the two of you."

"You're right. I'm pretty sure her mother is going to put the blame on my shoulders, though." He straightened. "But I'm okay with that."

"You are?" His father didn't sound surprised. Instead, it

sounded like he was simply encouraging Kyle to talk more. That was strange but good, too. He needed to talk about everything he was feeling. Even if it wasn't right or even if he should have known better, Kyle knew he needed to talk about what he was feeling at the very least.

"I'm older, and the man," he said slowly, pausing a moment to gauge his father's reaction. But his father was simply staring at him.

Waiting for him to continue.

Feeling like a child again, Kyle fumbled through his explanation some more. "I . . . I should have known better."

"Hmm," Daed murmured.

Okay. So he hadn't given the

consequences of what they were doing a whole lot of thought. But, he also had two older brothers, one of whom was engaged, and the other recently married. Though neither of them talked about their private lives with their women, Kyle knew he could have asked either of them about birth control. They might have lectured him, but they would have spoken to him frankly.

Sure, it would have been really uncomfortable, but it would have been easier than what they were going through now.

"When are you going to speak to Gabby's mother?"

"Whenever Gabby is ready."

"I'm thinking the sooner the better is best, son," his father said.

Eager to get it over with, Kyle nodded. "I agree."

Daed stood up. *"Gut."* Resting a hand on Kyle's shoulder, he said, "You should go rescue Gabby from your mother's clutches now. If we're not careful, your mother will soon be discussing cradles and high chairs with the poor girl, and I don't think she's quite prepared for that yet."

After shooting a grateful look in his father's direction, Kyle strode toward the kitchen. What a morning the Lord had in store for him! He'd started out thinking about bags of feed and ended it realizing that he was going to be a father in a few short months.

Six

"Instead of going home, I hid in an abandoned tree house in the woods by the Kurtzes' farm."

Jimmy had never seen their house in such disarray. Mamm was cleaning and scrubbing anything that didn't move, Daed was suddenly working on a porch swing, and everyone else was tiptoeing around them.

Except for Kyle. Kyle was holed up in his room and hadn't come out for hours.

"What's going on around here, Jimmy?" Betty asked when she found him in the tack room of the barn. "Mamm and Daed are working like the bishop is on his way over, Harley ran out of here after talking to Kyle, and every time I knock on Kyle's door, he tells me to leave him alone."

Jimmy didn't know how to answer her. He knew whatever was going on had to do with Kyle and Gabby, but he had no idea what, exactly, the problem was. And since he'd already said too much to Kyle that morning, he was hesitant to speculate anymore. "I didn't know Kyle let Harley in his room," he murmured. "He told me to go away when I knocked." Of course, he'd probably deserved Kyle's cold shoulder, but it had still stung.

Betty groaned. "That's all you have to report?"

Jimmy grinned at her choice of words. *Report* indeed. "Being told off by my little brother felt pretty important to me."

His sister folded her arms across her chest and tapped her foot. "You are missing the point, Jimmy. There's a crisis going on in the middle of our house and you and I are stuck out in the dark. We need to find out what has happened to Kyle."

"I'm thinking Beth probably don't know what's going on, either."

"Beth is nannying. She can't help but be out of the loop."

Jimmy knew his youngest sister had a point. Their sister, Beth, was a busy nanny for an English couple. She even spent the night over at their house one or two times a week. All he was trying to do was calm down the most excitable member of the family. Experience had taught him that whenever Betty was riled up, everyone else was going to be riled up, too.

"I don't know what to tell ya, Betty. We'll find out what happened when the time is right, I reckon."

"Whatever that means," she murmured with a groan. Still looking like a struggling detective, she peered out of the small window of the tack room. "Daed looks intent but not angry. What do you think that means?"

"There ain't no telling."

"You say that because you haven't caught sight of his expression." She waved a hand. "Come over and see for yourself."

"*Nee.* I'm not going to spy on Daed."

"But —"

It was time to finish up this silly, speculative conversation. "Betty, you know as well as I do that our parents just had a talk with Kyle and Gabby. They probably told them to break up and Kyle's upset."

Her eyes widened. "Do you really think they would've said that? Kyle likes Gabby a lot."

"What else could they have said?"

After a pause, he decided to share some more. "I told Kyle this morning that he needed to end things with Gabby because they were too different."

"Was that before or after Kyle was kissing her on the picnic table?"

"Before."

She smiled. "I don't think he listened to ya, Jimmy."

Thinking of how Kyle had been locked in an embrace more passionate than he and Sarah had ever experienced, he nodded. "That's for sure. But that's probably why Mamm and Daed talked to him. He needs to behave better." He nodded, thinking everything he said was making perfect sense.

Betty still looked skeptical. "I

don't know, Jim. Daed doesn't usually start building swings after he gets mad at us . . ."

"If you're so concerned, go ask Daed yourself."

"You know what? I just might." She turned away and walked back out of the barn.

Against his will, he peeked out the window. And, to his shock, she went right over to their father and started talking to him.

Jimmy held his breath, sure she was going to get a talking-to about her behavior as well. But instead, their father neatly placed his tools on the ground then sat down beside Betty.

Still watching like a Peeping Tom, Jimmy scratched his head. Things really were out of sorts around the house.

Ten minutes later, Betty glanced toward the window where he was lurking, raised her chin, and then walked into the house. Which meant now everyone but him and Beth knew what was going on.

After their father went inside, too, Jimmy couldn't sit in the tack room another moment.

Feeling out of sorts, he decided to take a break and go see Sarah. If he told her everything, she would likely have some good advice. Or, at the very least, she would make him feel better.

After hitching up the buggy, he guided Vixen down the road to Sarah's house. The day was clear and the air was crisp and cool. Bracing. Passing a farm that had a large Christmas wreath attached to its entrance, he couldn't help but smile. This truly was the season of hope. He almost felt better with every yard they passed.

An hour later, Jimmy was wondering if Sarah would ever be able to make him feel better. He'd found her cutting out a new dress and she hadn't looked especially excited to stop what she was doing to talk to him.

When he'd suggested they go sit together on her parents' front porch, she'd grudgingly followed him outside but had chosen to sit on one of the front steps instead of next to him on the porch swing.

After he'd filled her in on all the excitement around his house, she hadn't looked all that interested.

Actually, she'd looked kind of bored.

"I think you're making mountains out of molehills," she finally said.

"Sarah, you know my parents almost as well as I do. We both know there's no way they were happy with Kyle kissing his *Englischer* girlfriend in our front yard."

"I don't think they are as shocked as you are making them out to be." She pursed her lips, then added, "Think about Harley and Katie."

"What about them?"

"They rushed to marry."

"So . . ."

"Katie told me that Harley had been real anxious for their wedding day."

"Well, yes. I mean they'd known each other a long time."

"You are missing the point," she said, sounding mighty impatient. "They were in love. No, they *are* in love."

He pulled on his collar. "Sarah, I'm getting the feeling you aren't just talking about Harley and Katie. Or Kyle."

Her cool demeanor that he'd always admired broke in two. "Oh, do you think so, Jimmy?"

Her voice was thick with sarcasm. He wasn't stupid, he knew what she was referring to. But what he didn't understand was why she thought he was the only reason they'd been postponing their wedding date.

"If you have something to say, I think you should say it."

"Fine. I've been starting to wonder if we should break up."

"What? *Nee!*"

She continued in her quiet, matter-of-fact voice, as if he hadn't uttered a single word of protest. "Over the last couple of days, I've been doing a lot of thinking and praying."

"About?"

"Jimmy, I'm sure it's as obvious to you as it is to me that there is a reason we haven't been rushing to the altar."

No, it had not been obvious to him. Not at all. Feeling like he'd gotten a punch to the gut, he tried to make her see reason. "Sarah, we've been waiting because your mother had cancer. That's what you wanted to do, *jah*? You didn't want your parents to worry about anything except for her health."

Hurt filled her gaze. "All of that happened last year."

Jimmy contemplated pointing out that it had only been a few months since her mother had been given a clean bill of health. Her father had also complained about the expensive doctor bills. Jimmy had assumed that they were now waiting until those bills were paid off. "A lot has still been happening. We've been waiting until things quieted down."

"I know, but I think there has been something else going on." She lifted her chin. "I think we could name a lot of reasons why we haven't married yet, but I don't think any of them are the complete reason we haven't gone to the altar."

"What do you think it is?"

"I think we've been stuck in a rut."

"What is that supposed to mean?"

"It means we haven't been going forward. You know . . . slowly drifting backward," she continued, as if he didn't know what being stuck in a rut meant.

"If we've been stuck, we can become unstuck."

"I don't think so. I see no way out of this if we stay together."

If? Feeling like they were talking about two different things, he said, "Sarah, we might have been stuck, but we've also been making plans."

"Yes, we have, but nothing concrete. Nothing that has been lasting."

"You know what? We can set a date now. We can get married as soon as you want to."

"That is the problem, Jimmy. We shouldn't 'have' to set a date as soon as 'I want to.' Something is missing, and I think it's time for us to at last admit that whatever it is, it isn't likely to be found."

Looking at her serene expression,

watching the way she was position-
ing her body so she wasn't even
completely facing him, he felt betrayed. "I think you've been plan-
ning this for some time," he said.
"I think you've been unhappy for a
while and have been just biding
your time until you came up with
something else, or someone else."
Jumping on that excuse, he blurted,
"Is that what happened, Sarah?
Have you found another man?"

"*Nee.* This isn't about needing a
man to marry me, Jimmy. It's about
wanting to have something special.
It's about wanting you to love me."

"But I do." When she stared at
him expectantly, like she was hoping for something more, he added,
"You knew that, Sarah."

She sighed. "I think I need more words than that."

"More words?"

"I want us to be so in love that we don't want to wait another two months — or another two years — to marry."

"Good relationships aren't all about being anxious and impatient." Inwardly, he winced. It was doubtful that he could sound more prudish.

"That is true. But I think that it's okay to want some of that, too, though. Don't you think that a little bit of romance and impatience can be a *gut* thing?"

"Maybe. I mean, I guess so." He inhaled as he heard his words. Even to his ears, they had sounded awfully lackluster.

She looked disappointed, like yet again he'd failed whatever test she'd hoped he would pass.

"When you're sure, let me know." She walked to her front door. "Until then, I think we might need to take a break for a while," she whispered before stepping inside.

He couldn't help but notice that she hadn't spared him a backward glance.

"I'm trying to be honest, Sarah. There's nothing wrong with that, right?" he asked to the closed door. But, of course, she hadn't heard him.

Though, maybe they hadn't actually heard each other for some time. Or worse, they hadn't even tried to listen.

If that had happened, then that would be the saddest thing of all.

SEVEN

"I was sure I was going to see the Eight do something outlandish or bad. But all they did was have a campfire and toast s'mores and laugh a lot."

"That will be one hundred twenty-four, thirty-eight," Gabby said to the customer as she finished bagging the woman's groceries.

"Those lamb chops add up, don't they?" the lady said as she swiped her credit card on the machine.

"Yes, ma'am. But they're good

though."

"They really are," she replied as she put the three canvas totes back in her cart. "Have a nice day, Gabby."

"You, too." Gabby smiled at her before turning to check out the next customer. But then she realized that her line was momentarily empty.

Thank goodness for that. For at least a few minutes, she could lean against the counter and relax. Even doing such a small thing made her feel better.

She'd been on her shift for seven hours, and she'd had only two short breaks and a half-hour lunch. Usually she loved busy days at Walnut Creek Cheese Shop. It made the time go by fast and kept her mind off her usual problems and worries.

But today had been exhausting. For the last hour, it had been a struggle to keep smiling. She didn't know if it was because of her pregnancy . . . or the fact that Kyle was coming to meet her at four o'clock and go home with her so they could tell her mother and Lane about the baby.

The baby. It still didn't seem real, almost like it was just an idea that she should be afraid about.

But maybe that was part of why everything seemed so strange. After yesterday's visit to Kyle's house, she wasn't all that afraid about the future anymore. Oh, sure, she was scared to tell her mom and going to be embarrassed for Lane and her friends to find out, but Kyle had been amazing and so supportive. Even his parents hadn't acted like she was a terrible person. Instead, they'd swallowed their shock and asked how she was feeling.

She could only hope that her mother would be an eighth as nice about the news.

"Gabby, time to sign out," Laura, the manager, said as she approached. "We'll see you in two days."

"Great. Thank you."

"No, thank you. You've turned into a great cashier."

"Thanks." Gabby didn't take that praise lightly. Learning the job had been a lot harder than she thought it would be. There was a bit of pressure doing it, too. The first couple of times she'd been at the checkout on her own, she'd messed up, causing a whole line of people to get irritated. Now she was almost as quick as Jeff, who was the head cashier and had worked at the shop for ten years.

After turning in her receipts and cash drawer, she hurried over to the staff's break room, anxious to take off her apron.

Just as she turned the corner, Alaina winked at her. "Your Amish guy is here already."

"Really? Where?"

She nodded toward the side door. "He's over there talking with those two couples."

Looking to where Alaina was pointing, Gabby grinned. Yep, there was Kyle, looking relaxed and happy. He was talking to a couple of his brother's friends, too. She knew Kyle well enough to know about the Eight and their close friendship.

For a moment, she considered walking up to them to tell Kyle that she'd be right out but elected to wait. A trip to the bathroom was in order, and she wanted to brush her hair before she saw him, too.

Minutes later, when she was running a brush through her long hair, she stared at herself in the mirror, wondering if she looked different yet. And how all of her was going to change. Was she ready for the changes? She didn't know.

Sometimes all the changes that were about to happen really did feel overwhelming.

She braided her hair in a loose plait and secured it, then grabbed her purse and headed back to where she saw Kyle last. He was alone now and was looking for her.

The moment he spied her, he smiled. "Hey. You snuck out on me. One minute, I saw you ringing out a lady, and the next, you were gone."

"When I got off my shift I saw that you were talking to your brother's friends. I decided to get cleaned up real fast."

"Logan, Tricia, Katie, and Will

were here."

"I like how you're friends with them, too."

"I've known them since we were all small. Sometimes I feel like I don't have just one older sister and two older brothers, I've got a whole mess of them."

"I bet. At least they're nice."

"Yep. They're *gut.* So, are ya ready?"

She nodded. "I've got the car today, so we can drive."

"I'm glad of that. It's cold out."

"It is." After they got in, she blasted the heat, and when they got out onto the highway, he said, "How are you?"

She knew what he meant. "Scared. I don't think my mom is

going to handle the news as well as your parents did."

He didn't look surprised. "I know. Don't take this the wrong way, but it doesn't matter."

"What?"

"I've been thinking a lot about this. I mean, us, and . . . Gabby, it's you and me now. We're a pair. My concern is about you and me, not making your mother like me or even if she will accept the fact that we're going to have a baby."

How had she gotten so lucky? Gabby couldn't imagine another eighteen-year-old on the planet being so caring and mature. "You really mean that, don't you?"

He nodded. "I'm not going to pretend I have all the answers, but

I do know that you and this baby are my main concerns right now."

As she parked the car in front of her small house, Gabby released a deep breath of air. She didn't know if she felt better about the upcoming conversation with her mother, but at least she didn't feel as alone. That had to count for something. "Let's go get this over with, then."

An hour later, Gabby knew she would pay someone a hundred dollars if he or she could get her out of the room fast. She'd just experienced the longest forty minutes of her entire life.

To say her mom hadn't taken the news well was an understatement. She was livid. The only silver lining in the whole situation — and she wasn't even sure it could be called a silver lining — was that her mother wasn't putting all the blame on Kyle's shoulders.

No, she was bestowing that gift on Gabby.

"How could you be so stupid?" she asked for at least the fifth time. "I thought you were smarter than this."

Gabby knew better than to try to explain herself. Instead she stayed silent and prayed that her mother would calm down soon. Really soon.

Unfortunately her silence seemed to only make her mother more livid. "Nothing? You don't have a thing to say?"

"I don't have anything to say that you want to hear."

"This was my fault, Mrs. Ferrara," Kyle interjected.

"It's not Missus," she said in a cold tone of voice. "It's Ms."

"All right . . ."

"And this most certainly is Gabby's fault. She knows what happened to me. She knew better than to have sex without promises. And better than to count on someone like you."

This was getting even worse. "Mother, you can't talk like that to Kyle."

"It's my house. I'll speak to him however I want to." Standing up, her mom began to pace again. "Have you even thought about how you're going to afford this baby, Gabrielle?"

"Not yet."

"Is that because you expect me to foot the bill?"

"I graduated, Mom. I have a job."

"You have a job at a grocery store. That's not going to pay for much."

"Gabby ain't alone," Kyle said. "I'll help her pay for anything the babe needs."

She stopped pacing long enough to send Kyle a scathing look. "Like that makes me feel any better."

A muscle in Kyle's jaw ticked. It was obvious he was trying to stay respectful, but he was just about at the end of his limit.

Oh, this was terrible. Gabby had known that her mom was going to flip out, but she hadn't expected her mother to start saying hateful things to Kyle's face and bringing up money.

Her mother paced again. "About the only positive thing I can say is that I'm impressed he's here."

Kyle lifted his chin. "I'm not going anywhere."

"Just wait until your parents find out. They'll put a stop to your relationship then."

"We told them yesterday," Kyle said before Gabby could warn him not to mention that. "They aren't pleased, but they don't want me to break up with Gabby or anything."

Her mother paused in midstride. "They found out *yesterday?*" Before Kyle could reply, she spun to face Gabby. "When?"

"Yesterday morning." She shrugged. "Does it even matter?"

Just like she'd feared, her mother went on the offensive. "So they got to find out first? Why is that?"

Kyle was looking at her mother like she was unhinged.

Though Gabby couldn't blame him, she tried to smooth things over. "Mom, it's not like it was a race. I went over to tell Kyle and he wanted to tell his parents right away."

"Why did you wait until today to tell me?"

Gabby knew there was a thick thread of hurt in her mother's voice, but at the moment, she couldn't care less about that. Getting to her feet, she said, "This isn't about you."

"Of course it is. I got knocked up by an Amish boy and then abandoned, Gabby. You knew how this news was going to affect me." She shook her head. "And how are you going to be able to tell Lane? No, what are we going to tell your brother about how this happened?"

"Gee, I don't know. Probably that I had sex with my boyfriend and got pregnant."

Looking even more furious, her mother marched up to her. "Watch your mouth."

"*You* watch your mouth," Gabby retorted. "I'm trying to talk to you. You're the one who is being so hateful."

"Gabrielle — enough!" She raised her hand.

To do what, Gabby wasn't sure. Her mother had never hit her, but at the moment it didn't seem like she was being herself.

Before she knew what to do, Kyle stood up and stepped right in front of her. "Don't touch her."

"What is going on?" Lane said from the front doorway. "Mom? Kyle? Gabby?" As he took in everyone's position in the room, he started toward her. "Gabby, are you all right?"

"Go to your room, Lane," Mom called out.

"Uh, I don't think so." He walked to Gabby's side. "Why are all of you so angry?"

Gabby knew there was no sense in delaying the inevitable. "You might as well find out now. I found out I'm pregnant and we just told Mom."

Lane's expression went slack. "Oh, wow."

"That's one way of putting it," her mother said.

"Can we calm down now?" Kyle asked.

Her mother was literally shaking, she looked so mad. Pointing a finger at Kyle, she said, "I want you out of here. Now."

But Kyle didn't move. Instead, he stared at Gabby. "What do you want me to do?"

"Stay."

"Then I'll stay."

Relief poured through her. Kyle really was amazing. Here her mother was being completely terrible, but he was simply standing next to her, so calm and stalwart, making sure Gabby realized that his only concern was for her. "Thanks," she whispered.

"No, this is not how it's going to go," her mother said. "Gabby, there's only one way for me to forgive you. You are going to say goodbye to him and promise to never see him again."

"That's not going to happen." And why did her mom think Gabby owed her an apology anyway?

"That's your only option."

Lane cleared his throat, signaling to Gabby that he was just as shocked as she was by how miserable their mother was being. "You know what? We ought to sit down."

"No," Mom blurted. "He needs to leave."

Gabby shook her head. "Mother, his name is Kyle, and I need him here."

"If you don't do what I'm telling you to do, then you need to leave, Gabrielle."

"You're going to kick me out?"

"No, you're going to be making that choice."

Lane strode forward. "Mom, you really need to calm down. You can't just go and kick Gabby out."

"I can and I will." She folded her hands across her chest. "What's it going to be, Gabby?"

She was hurt and scared and feeling betrayed. For years, she'd taken care of herself, taken care of Lane, and their house. In a lot of ways, she'd even taken care of their mother.

But it all came down to whether or not she wanted to continue to live this way — or if she wanted to bring her baby up in this environment.

And if that was the case, then there really wasn't any choice. She looked at Kyle. He was standing still, and his face was a mask. But when she caught his eye, he nodded.

All right, then. "Mom, if you're going to make me choose, then I guess I'll be leaving."

"Gabby." Lane's voice was hoarse. "What are you doing?"

She turned to her younger brother, who now stood almost a full foot taller than she was. Their eyes met. She hoped there was some way he was going to be able to read her expression and would understand that she had no choice. "I . . . I'm sorry, Lane. You know that I love you, right? That no matter what happens, I'll always be there for you?" When he nodded, she breathed a sigh of relief. "I'll call you soon, but I have to leave."

"I know." Lane's voice was thick with emotion but resigned.

Walking to Kyle's side, she murmured, "I need to get my things. Would you come to my room and help me pack?"

"Of course. I'll do whatever you need," he said.

She paused, half-hoping that her mother would change her mind. But her mom turned away.

Now that the decision was made, Gabby walked to her room, Kyle on her heels.

She was leaving home.

She couldn't believe it.

But maybe she actually could.

EIGHT

"Just when they were leaving, Harley tamped down the fire, and the woods turned black. I got scared and scrambled down the tree. But then one of the branches broke and I got stuck."

Kyle had called Harley's friend Marie, who had recently married another one of the Eight, John Byler.

Minutes after they'd gone into Gabby's room, he'd known they were going to need some help.

Gabby had started scurrying around her room, throwing clothes and a hundred other items into two duffle bags. He'd stood helplessly to the side and watched, unable to offer any words of comfort or advice.

Unable to help her sort through her personal items.

All he'd been sure of was that she had too much stuff to carry.

And so he'd picked up her phone and called the one phone number he had memorized: Marie's. Luckily, she'd picked up the phone right away and, after hearing his stilted explanation, had promised that she and John B. would be at Gabby's house within thirty minutes.

They'd done just that, texting

Gabby when they were parked on the street.

When Gabby had opened her bedroom door, the house had been silent. Neither her mother nor Lane had been there.

Gabby, who'd been valiantly fighting off tears, seemed shocked by that. After a moment, she pulled her key ring out of her purse and set it on the kitchen counter.

"Do you not need any of those keys?"

"No."

"All right." Still, he felt strange, just escorting her out. "Do you want to write a note or something?"

For the first time in the hour, a smidgen of humor lit her eyes. "I don't think there's much left to say,

Kyle."

"Let's go, then."

They walked outside. John got out of Marie's truck when he spied them and helped put the bags in the back.

When Gabby and Kyle sat down in the backseat, Marie turned to them. "Where to?"

There was only one place he knew to go, and that was his house. But he knew Gabby needed a few minutes before facing his family.

"I'm not sure," he said at last. "Could we . . . I mean, I know you probably have a lot to do, but could we drive around or something?"

"Are you two hungry?" Marie asked. "We could drive over to Sugarcreek and get some food.

There's a good sandwich place there."

"What do you think?" he whispered to Gabby.

She nodded. "That sounds good. Thanks, Marie."

Marie smiled before pulling away from the curb and driving. After asking a few questions about their comfort, making sure they had enough warm air blowing on them on the backseat, John kept quiet.

Gabby closed her eyes, looking relieved for the silence.

Kyle felt like he could finally pause for a moment and take a deep breath. For the last two hours, he'd been so tense, he'd felt like he could break in two. Now that there was nothing they could do except wait, it was like a giant boulder had just slid off his shoulders.

He forced himself to think only of Gabby and their immediate concerns instead of letting their whole situation get the best of him.

When they got to the sandwich shop, they all got out and placed their orders. John and Marie insisted on paying for their meals.

Then they all took their seats in a booth in the back of the small restaurant.

Kyle had ordered a turkey club. His first bite tasted so good. It tasted even better when he noticed that Gabby was eating her food, too. She was an independent woman, but he still felt pleased to see that he was helping her take care of herself.

When they were about halfway done, the door opened at the front and Harley and Beth walked through. As soon as they spied them, Harley waved a hand, then placed their order.

"John, how did Harley know we were here?" Kyle asked.

"I called Will at work and asked him to track Harley down." He shrugged. "I'm guessing he got ahold of your sister next."

"It was that easy?" Gabby asked. She knew enough about Harley to know that he rarely used a cell phone and that Beth worked at an *Englischer*'s home.

Marie smiled at Gabby. "You'll learn that we Eight have our own methods of getting ahold of each other."

"That sounds impressive, and kind of sneaky."

Marie chuckled. "I don't know about that. But I do know that we know each other so well we've learned to not let just any old obstacle get in our way."

"*Jah.* Where there's a will, there's a way," John supplied.

Gabby raised her eyebrows. "Now I'm even more impressed."

"You should be," Marie teased. "But don't worry. I'm more than happy to share my methods. Before you know it, you'll be getting hold of Kyle at any time of day without a problem."

The others laughed.

Their camaraderie and willingness to make Gabby feel at ease was a blessing. She was talking more, laughing more, and much of the tension that she'd been displaying was inching away right before his eyes. Kyle was glad about that.

Though he attempted to smile, he knew he was managing to only look sick. But it couldn't be helped. Every part of him was on pins and needles as he watched his brother and sister wait for their sandwiches.

What were they going to say to him? He really hoped neither would embarrass Gabby in public.

John B.'s palm on his shoulder brought him out of his reverie. "Don't think the worst," he murmured. "Harley sounded worried about you, not mad."

He exhaled. "I hope you're right."

"I am."

"Gabby, I hope you don't mind me showing up with Harley, but I couldn't stay away," Beth said as she scooted in next to Gabby and then pulled her into a quick, fierce hug. "I'm so sorry about what's happened."

"Thanks," Gabby said. She looked Kyle's way before looking down at her feet again.

Kyle knew she was embarrassed about the whole situation.

Before he could try to comfort her, Harley spoke again. "Hey, now. Try not to look so glum. We're family now, *jah*?"

Her eyes widened. "Well . . ."

"Come now. You're making me an uncle and Beth an aunt."

John, who had been just about to take a bite of his sandwich, put it back on the plate. "You're pregnant?"

"*Jah,*" Kyle said.

Marie blinked before recovering quickly. "Congratulations."

"Thank you," Gabby said with a watery smile. "I don't know what to think right now. I mean, I guess it's not good —"

"It is," Harley said. "Regrets don't get you far, Gabby."

When Gabby looked even more mystified, Kyle slipped a hand under the table and took hold of hers. Of course they weren't fooling anyone, but he had a feeling that the last thing Gabby wanted was for him to make more of a public spectacle of their relationship.

Then he filled everyone in. "We told Gabby's mother today. She didn't take the news well."

"What happened?" Beth asked.

"She kicked me out," Gabby shared.

John looked at her sadly. "I'm sorry. Maybe she'll come around?"

"I doubt it."

"No offense, but I bet as soon as she realizes what a blessing a baby is, your mother will come around."

"I don't think so. She's not just upset about the baby. It's the fact that I love Kyle."

"Kyle is a good man," Harley said.

"It's that he's Amish. My mother . . ." Gabby took a fortifying breath, waving his hand away when he tried to interrupt. "My mother had a relationship with an Amish boy when she was a teenager. She also got pregnant, but the boy abandoned her."

"Was it an Amish man in the community?"

"I think so. I mean, I don't know. She never told me his name."

"So you're half Amish."

"*Nee,* she ain't," John protested. "I can't imagine that any man who was baptized in the faith would do such a thing."

"Just because a man says he's a believer doesn't mean he is good. Maybe he was a real jerk," Beth said. "It can happen, you know."

Kyle hated the worry on Gabby's face. "Look, all of this discussion isn't helping Gabby at all," he said. "Let's drop it."

"No, I . . . well, I don't think I mind," Gabby said softly. Looking at all of them, she smiled. "Just a few minutes ago, I was thinking that the worst thing I could have imagined happening actually did. I got pregnant without being married — and as a teenager. The father is a part of the community my mother doesn't like, and now I've been kicked out of my house . . ."

"Gabby . . ."

"But now, well, I'm thinking that while all of those things are true, it's not all that is true. God has also been working to show me that all isn't lost." She lifted her chin. "I still have my brother's love and support." Turning to Kyle, she added, "And Kyle and our baby and even a little bit of hope. I'm grateful for that."

"You also have all of us," Marie said. "I know you don't know John and me, but I promise you, our pasts aren't without a little bit of drama, too. We also love Kyle's older brother, which means that we love Kyle, which means that we love you, too."

"It's as easy as that?"

"God loves us all. So, yes. It's just that easy."

"What about me?" Beth asked, a

smile in her voice. "I'm Harley's sister."

John shrugged. "Sorry, Beth. We Eight only promised to love *some* members of each other's families."

They all burst into laughter as Beth picked up a potato chip and tossed it at him.

Moments later, when Kyle noticed Gabby was only moving around the food on her plate, he knew it was time. "Ready?" he asked.

Her eyes widened, but she nodded. "Yes."

"We'd better get out of here," Kyle said.

Harley stood up as well. "Where are you going?"

"Home. Gabby and I need to get

her settled."

Gabby looked terrified. "I don't know, Kyle. Maybe . . ."

Harley shook his head. "No, Kyle is definitely right. It's time you went home. To your new home," he said meaningfully.

His brother's tone, if not his words, rang in Kyle's ears the whole way to his house.

Nine

"So I started calling out to Harley. Actually, I started yelling all their names. Will Kurtz got to me first."

One Week Later

Gabby had known moving into the Lambrights' house was going to feel strange. And it did.

What she hadn't counted on, however, was that it would also feel so comforting. William and Emma Lambright had a steady way about them that made Gabby feel more relaxed. Both liked their routines and to keep everyone else in the house on track, too.

And while their children — Betty especially — seemed to find it annoying, Gabby found it to be a relief. She loved knowing what to expect. It had been a very long time since Gabby had felt like she only needed to worry about herself. For once she wasn't having to worry about picking up Lane from football practice or finding the time to run to the grocery store. She wasn't having to wonder if her mother was going to be home for supper or wonder how she was going to avoid the boys two houses down.

Now, all she had to do was ask Mrs. Lambright how she could help with a chore and then do as she asked. It felt exhilarating.

Kyle's parents also were even-tempered. They didn't get excited or stressed-out about much, perhaps because they were so used to managing their five grown children. Gabby figured that was why, even though she knew Mr. and Mrs. Lambright weren't exactly pleased about the pregnancy, they seemed to take it in stride. Neither acted like Gabby was an interloper in their home or glared at her when she didn't understand something someone said.

In addition, Mrs. Lambright talked about the baby all the time, just as if it was the most natural thing in the world for their youngest son to be giving them their first grandchild.

Kyle's siblings' interactions with her had also been a surprise. Though she wouldn't say that they went out of their way to befriend her, neither did they make her feel like an unwanted guest. As soon as they knew that Gabby wanted to do her fair share of helping around the house, Betty and Beth took turns showing her how to help do laundry, garden, and cook in their Amish home.

However, Gabby's biggest surprise was Mr. Lambright himself.

She'd known from hearing Kyle — as well as her other interactions with Mr. Lambright — that he wasn't the most humorous or chattiest of men.

In addition, his resting expression was pretty foreboding. He had ice-blue eyes that seemed to watch everything intently. He kind of reminded her of one of those gray wolves she'd seen on the National Geographic channel.

She'd actually been trembling when Kyle told his parents about Gabby's mother kicking her out of the house. Mr. Lambright's expression had turned so foreboding that she'd wanted to be anywhere but standing in front of him. Then, she'd yearned to simply disappear when he turned and walked away without saying a word.

Though Kyle had told her not to worry, she had. It had taken everything she had not to burst into tears when Mrs. Lambright led her to the empty *dawdi haus* — the attached grouping of rooms that Kyle's grandparents had once occupied — and helped Gabby make up the bed in the bedroom. She'd been sure his parents were wishing they'd never opened their home to her.

However, when Gabby entered the kitchen quietly the next morning, she'd discovered Kyle's father sitting alone at the very big table sipping coffee.

The moment he spied her, he stood up. "Ah, Gabby. There you are."

It was ten after seven in the morning. She had a feeling she was the last to wake up. "I'm sorry, did I sleep too late?"

He raised one eyebrow. "At seven? *Nee.*" He smiled slightly. "No, I've been waiting for you."

She sat down, telling herself that whatever he had to say, she could take it. He and Mrs. Lambright had given her a place to live when her own mother had not.

But still she found herself clenching her hands in anticipation of what was to come.

He cleared his throat. "So, um, how did you sleep?"

How did she sleep? "Good. I mean, I slept well." When he simply stared at her, she said, "What about you?"

He looked taken aback. "Me?" After a pause, he rubbed the back of his neck. "Well, um, to be honest, I didn't sleep all that good."

"I'm sorry to hear that."

"It can't be helped, I suppose. The older I get, the less the Lord seems to want me to have a good night's rest." He smiled at her.

This was the strangest of conversations! Awkwardly, she smiled back.

"Gabby, I wanted to speak to you about what happened."

"Yes?"

"Well, when you and Kyle told Emma and me the news? I have to tell ya, it made me pretty upset."

Here it came. He was going to blame her for ruining Kyle and for getting pregnant. She looked down at her feet. "I know. But I promise

I didn't do it intentionally."

He gaped at her, then shook his head. "*Nee.* You misunderstand, child. I ain't talking about you having a baby. I'm talking about your mother treating you the way she did."

"Oh." She shifted uncomfortably.

"I'm sure your mother is a fine woman, but I don't understand how she could have cast you out."

Though Gabby didn't understand it either, she felt compelled to offer an explanation. "My mother, she still holds a lot of resentment because of the way my father refused to acknowledge her after he discovered she was pregnant." She paused, trying to soften the story her mother always told into something a little less mean-sounding. "I guess he kind of went into hiding in his community."

His eyes narrowed. "I don't understand how a man can go into hiding. How could that be?"

She gulped. "Um, I guess it was possible for him to do that eighteen years ago because he's Amish."

William's blue eyes widened. "Your father is Amish?" When she nodded, he leaned back in his chair. "My word. I didn't know that."

"Not many people do. My mother hated to talk about him, other than the fact he was Amish and that I should never date any Amish boys." In truth, she'd said more than that. Her mother had practically made her promise to not have anything to do with anyone who was Amish. Of course, she'd never done such a thing.

"Though that's very sad, I don't understand why she treated you so unfairly. After all, our Kyle didn't abandon you."

"You're right. From the moment I told Kyle about the baby, he's been supportive. Even though I'm sure he was just as shocked as I was, he stayed by my side." Smiling softly, she continued, "Your son has been nothing but wonderful to me."

Mr. Lambright looked a little embarrassed by her praise. After rubbing his hand on his beard, he said, "I find it ironic that your mother abandoned you even though she had been abandoned herself."

Gabby thought that was pretty ironic, too. Her mother's actions didn't make a lot of sense. But admitting that seemed too hard. "I don't know what to say," she whispered.

"I don't reckon that you need to say anything at all. I just want you to understand that Emma and I will not forsake you. No matter what happens, we're going to be in this together."

"Thank you, Mr. Lambright."

"I'm thinking it's time you called me William. Don't you?"

"All right. Thank you, William."

His blue eyes brightened as he smiled. "Now, let's get you something to eat." He stood up and walked to the oven and pulled out a plate that Emma had obviously placed there for her. "I hope you like pancakes."

"I love them," she said with a smile. "This was so nice of Emma to leave them for me. I really am sorry I didn't get up earlier."

"Don't apologize for resting, child. Now, get your plate."

Taking the plate from him, she attempted to make a dent in the stack of five pancakes.

William sipped coffee and shared a funny story about when Kyle had gotten stuck in a tree when he was a little boy. As she ate and listened to his deep voice, Gabby felt another layer of worry slip off her shoulders. In the midst of what she'd thought were the darkest days of her life, she was actually finding a lot of wonderful moments.

She was being accepted and taken care of.

And, for the first time in her life, she was getting a taste of what it must be like to have a father. And that alone felt like something precious and sweet.

A perfect, unexpected gift.

Ten

"It took Will, Andy, and Harley a good thirty minutes to get me out of that tree. Then, after I got to the ground, E.A. and Katie gave me hugs. I was embarrassed — and scared of what Harley was going to tell Mamm and Daed when we got home."

Ever since Gabby had moved into the *dawdi haus,* Kyle had felt like he was balancing precariously on a fraying tightrope. On one side of the rope were all his worries about

Gabby. He knew she had to be feeling like a fish out of water over in the *dawdi haus*. Gabby had never had to live without electricity or the Internet. She didn't know Pennsylvania Dutch and wasn't used to being around so many farm animals.

He felt like he was constantly on patrol whenever she was near, trying to help her get acclimated to a lifestyle she'd never intended on living.

On the other side of the tightrope was his whole family. His parents, though kind and patient to her, made it known to him that they were more than a little disappointed in him. They'd raised him to value marriage and had expected him to follow the rules of both the church and the family — one of which was to not have sex before marriage.

Then there were his siblings. While they, again, seemed to get along just fine with Gabby and acted genuinely happy about the baby, it was obvious that having a new English girl living with them wasn't easy.

Especially not for Jimmy.

"Where is Gabby?" Jimmy asked early one morning about three weeks after she'd settled in.

Jimmy, Kyle, and their parents were all sitting around the kitchen table. Like always, Kyle and Jimmy had gotten up at five to see to the livestock in the barn while their mother had made breakfast.

This was usually the calmest time of the day. The most urgent needs of the farm had been noted or taken care of, and they'd always taken a good hour to enjoy breakfast and prepare for the rest of the day.

Which was why Jimmy's question had grated on Kyle. "I'm guessing she's still asleep in her room," he said.

"Does she know she's in an Amish home? She shouldn't be lazing about."

"I'm fairly sure she realizes she's in an Amish home, brother," Kyle replied. "And she's not lazing about. She's sleeping."

"I would have thought she would want to make herself useful, seeing as she has made herself at home here."

"Gabby has not only still been working at Walnut Cheese, she's been helping Mamm and Betty with the housework and cooking."

"That's true, she has," Betty added before giving Jimmy a dark look. "Not that the housework or kitchen is any concern of yours."

Jimmy cast Betty an irritated look. "All I'm saying is that I hope you've told her that we start our days early around here."

"It ain't your business what we discuss."

Mamm brought a plate filled with piping hot hash browns to the table. "I'm not sure where you're going with this, James."

"Nowhere. Simply making conversation."

Their father looked at him sharply but said nothing, just served himself some potatoes.

When their father had gotten his fill, both boys served themselves, then waited for their mother to sit down and fill her plate.

After each quietly bowed their heads in prayer, they picked up their forks.

Kyle had just taken a bite when Jimmy spoke again. "Do you know where you're going to live?"

"When?"

"You know. When the baby comes. Are you going to marry her soon?"

Kyle swallowed and took a sip of

juice. "That ain't none of your business."

"I think it is. I live here and I'm a part of the family." His voice hardened. "Why can't you answer me? Do you even know what you're going to do? Have you even truly thought about your future?" he pressed.

"I think it's pretty evident that I have," Kyle bit out.

"Well, what are you going to do?" When Kyle only gave him a dark look, Jimmy rolled his eyes. "You don't know, do you?"

"That's enough, Jimmy," Daed said. "You are purposely pestering your brother. That ain't right."

Kyle inhaled a sharp breath. Their father never bothered to explain himself.

But instead of backing down, Jimmy sighed. "Boy, it must be nice to be you, Kyle. If Harley or I had gotten some English girl with child, no one would be tiptoeing around so much."

"Jimmy, you are out of line," Daed said in Pennsylvania Dutch.

"Yes," Mamm said. "What in the world has gotten into you?"

"Nothing is wrong. Nothing at all."

"Something sure has," Betty muttered under her breath.

"Jimmy, I would have thought you'd be a lot more worried about your relationship with Sarah instead of what is going on with me," Kyle said.

"I would be more worried, if Sarah and I still had a relationship. We do not."

"What?" Betty asked.

"You heard me," Jimmy said. "Sarah broke up with me."

Kyle was so shocked, he didn't know where to look. "Oh."

"Oh?" Jimmy echoed. "Is that all you have to say?"

"How about that I'm sorry?" Kyle asked, doubting that even those words would make his brother feel better.

After casting a sympathetic look his way, their mother stood up. "James, when did this happen?"

"A few weeks ago."

"Maybe she will come around soon," Betty said.

"*Nee,* I don't think so. I think we are done." Looking even more morose, Jimmy sighed. "I *canna* believe I wasted so much time on her. I *canna* believe I've done everything right, lived here, helped with the farm, worked hard, dated a suitable girl, and now none of it seems to matter."

Kyle couldn't help but notice that he wasn't talking about love at all. "Maybe God intends for you to do something else."

"Is that what you think happened with you and Gabby? That God encouraged you to forget your honor with that girl?"

"Don't speak about Gabby like that. She isn't *that girl.* And she's been through more than you can imagine."

"Still, she's not suitable."

"She is for me."

"She —"

"She is right here," Gabby said from the doorway.

Everyone turned to stare at her. She had one hand braced against the wall, her hair in a ponytail, and was wearing a loose, modest-cut housedress. Plain white canvas sneakers were on her feet. Kyle thought she'd never looked prettier, or more vulnerable.

"Good morning, Gabby," Kyle said as he crossed the room to her side. Not caring that everyone was watching them, he leaned forward and kissed her brow. "How are you?"

She looked warily at Jimmy and his parents. "I'm okay." Looking down at her tennis shoes, she bit her lip. "I'm also embarrassed. I was relieved to have a place to stay, it never occurred to me that my being here was a problem for the rest of you."

"That's because it isn't," Betty said.

Gabby kept talking, as if she hadn't heard Betty's comment. "Jimmy, I can leave if you'd like me to."

Jimmy paled as he stood up. "I owe you an apology. I . . . well, I broke up with my fiancée and I am afraid I've been taking out my frustration on the rest of the family."

Gabby pursed her lips but said nothing.

And Kyle knew that there was nothing for her to say. Jimmy had hurt her feelings and made her feel unwelcome. And though it wasn't his fault, he felt responsible for it.

"Please sit down, dear," Mamm said. "It's time to eat some breakfast." She gestured to a plate of hot sausages in the center. "Perhaps you would like some sausage and eggs?"

Gabby's eyes widened, she looked a little green, and then, covering her mouth, she darted down the hall.

Kyle stepped toward her but glared at his brother first. "Jimmy, we've always been close and I've felt that I could always rely on you. But the way you spoke to Gabby this morning wasn't okay with me. I don't think it would be all right for any guest in our home." When Jimmy simply stared at him, Kyle hardened his voice. "I hope you figure things out real soon."

When Jimmy still didn't respond, Kyle turned away and walked down the hall. Hearing the water running in the bathroom, he tapped lightly on the door. "Gabby?"

"Yeah." She cleared her throat. "Um, I'll be out in a minute."

"Gabby, let me in," he said quietly.

"But —"

"Please."

After a few seconds passed, she

opened the door and stared at him. Her face was pale, and her eyes were watering. Hating to see her so upset, his heart went out to her. Stepping into the small space, he closed the door behind him.

To his surprise, he felt more comfortable in here with her than he had at the breakfast table.

"Now, what can I do to help?" he asked.

His heart started beating faster when she didn't answer right away.

Eleven

"But Harley said he wasn't going to be the one to tell Daed I was sneaking. That was my job. When I started whining, he looked at me right in the eye and said tonight likely wasn't going to be the last time I did something that I regretted. That whenever I did something wrong, I should own up to it."

"James, we need to talk, son. Now." Jimmy had rarely seen his father look so angry. Though his father rarely looked pleased about much, he usually kept a firm grip on his temper.

Today, though? His *daed* looked angry enough to spit nails.

Even worse was knowing that his anger was deserved.

"I'm sorry. I know I've been out of sorts this morning."

"*Nee.* Out of sorts is when one needs a second cup of *kaffi.* You have been deliberately disrespectful to both Kyle and to Gabby. That will not do."

"I know. Neither of them deserved what I said."

His father's thick gray eyebrows shot up. "*Deserve,* you say? Boy, I *canna* think of a time when anyone would deserve to be talked to the way you spoke to them."

"I know. I'll apologize. I'm not sure what is going on with me."

"I do. You are in a bad way because you don't know what to do about your own life."

Jimmy drew back. "Excuse me? I've been working on our farm all my life."

"I ain't talking about work. I'm talking about your heart." While Jimmy gaped at him, his father clucked his tongue. "James, you know what I am referring to. What are you ever going to do about Sarah?"

Even hearing her name made him feel desolate. He had no idea what he was going to do about her — or if there was anything to be done at all. "She and I aren't meant to be."

"Are you sure about that?" Mamm asked from the doorway. "You've known each other all your lives. You two fit together like peas in a pod. That means something, I think."

"I don't think so. Sarah asked me not to stop by her house anymore. She doesn't want to see me again."

His *daed* folded his arms over his chest. "And?"

"And nothing."

"Surely you aren't going to give up so easily."

"I'm not giving up, but what more can I do? A relationship takes two people."

His father looked at him closely. "Exactly. I'm thinking it's time you decided to work hard on patching things up with her."

Jimmy's first inclination was to protest that his father didn't know what he was talking about. That he was certain there wasn't any way to mend what had broken in his and Sarah's relationship.

But he caught himself in time. Thinking about how his little brother's eyes lit upon Gabby the moment he saw her, the way Kyle was even willing to run after her into the bathroom to be by her side? It humbled him.

Had he ever been willing to put himself in such a position like that? Had he ever been willing to do whatever it took to make things better for Sarah?

Making up his mind, he said, "I think I need to pay a call on Sarah today. I need to try."

"That's all you can do, *jah*?" his father said softly.

Gesturing down the hall to the still closed door, he said, "What should I do about Gabby and Kyle? I was almost unforgivably rude. Apologizing doesn't seem like it would be enough."

"You are right. You were rude. But 'almost' is the key word, don't you think, son?" Mamm asked. "What matters is that you say the words. We can all offer forgiveness and be forgiven, no matter what."

"I guess I could try."

She smiled at him, pure warmth filling her features. "*Jah, boo.*

That's what you should do."

Those words rang in his ears as he walked out to the barn to hitch up the buggy again. Everything with him and Sarah wasn't lost for good.

And even more importantly, he realized now that he couldn't bear for it to be lost for good. She was important to him, and he wanted her in his life. Now all he had to do was figure out how to make sure they both knew that.

An hour later, Jimmy knew he would always be glad that he'd listened to his parents. It took a lot of convincing, but he managed to convince Sarah to take a walk with him. She'd wanted to go someplace nearby, which meant they were walking in one of Sarah's family's fields. As romantic or perfect sites went, Jimmy reckoned it had a lot to be desired.

But perhaps it was better this way. The utilitarian area suited their relationship. Nothing about them had ever been full of grand gestures or exciting moments.

But, then again, those were things he had once thought weren't necessary. Instead, he'd yearned for something longer lasting and steadfast. Now he realized that it was possible to have both.

"Jimmy, what did you come over here to talk about?"

She sounded impatient, but she sounded anxious, too. As if she was hoping for him to say something special. With his mother's prodding still ringing in his ears, he spoke. "Sarah, I came over to tell you a lot of things. That I'm sorry I haven't been more attentive. That I wish I would've complimented you more and been more affectionate. I wish I would have asked you more about your days and talked about work less."

He paused for a breath. When he saw that she was still staring at him intently, he continued. "But, Sarah, most of all, I think the two of us deserve to work harder and fix our relationship. I think our future deserves that."

Her gaze softened. "I don't know if that's possible."

Looking at the fields, he smiled. These fields were much like their lives. Fitting symbols, even. "Sarah, do you remember back when we were just fourteen or fifteen?"

"Of course. What about it?"

She still had her guard up. He tried again. "I'm remembering the time just after we'd graduated school and we thought we were so old and mature."

Slowly she smiled. "My, but we were full of ourselves." She shook her head. "I was sure I knew everything back then."

"My father had already explained to me that I would have new jobs around the farm, but that I was also going to be allowed to have some extra time, too."

"So we could run around."

"But all I wanted to do was be with you," he murmured. "I thought you were the sweetest, most perfect girl I'd ever met."

Her eyes widened. "You never told me that."

"I didn't know how. Or maybe I was too afraid? But just because I never said the words didn't mean I never thought them." While she continued to stare at him in wonder, he said, "The reason I brought it up was because I remember the first time we sat together at a singing."

"And then after, you held my hand."

He nodded. "I felt like I had done something pretty amazing, getting you to settle on me."

She laughed softly. "I don't understand."

"You could have had anyone, Sarah. But you chose me."

Something new flickered in her eyes. "What do you think happened?"

"I'm not sure. Maybe I was so used to having you by my side, I stopped worrying about losing you?" He gestured to the fields. "Or, maybe, instead, we had to wait for the right time. Just like some years a field needs to rest in order to produce a good crop, maybe our relationship needed some time to settle and grow, too."

"It feels like it's taken a long time for us."

"Compared to Harley and Katie? Maybe, maybe not. They were friends for years before their romance blossomed."

"And your brother with the English girl?"

"Kyle and Gabby were meant to be together, I think. When I see them together, I realize they make sense. Even though everything about the two of them shouldn't work, it does. They're a good couple."

Before she could comment on that, he turned to face her and reached for both of her hands. "Sarah, I want us to try again. I want to stop worrying about the perfect time and be impulsive and just be together."

She looked up at him, hesitancy bright in her eyes. "I want a future with you. But do you think it's even possible?"

Because he had seen not only hesitancy but also longing in her gaze, he knew it was. After all this time, and after all the delays, the love that they had for each other was still there.

Feeling like he was finally following his heart instead of the doubts in his head, he cupped her cheeks in his hands and kissed her. Sarah inhaled sharply before relaxing against him and kissing him back with all the love and passion that he'd ever dreamed about.

After several long seconds, he pulled back, breathless.

And then smiled. "*Jah.* Sarah. I think a good and certain future between us is very possible. In fact, there is no doubt in my mind at all."

Sarah, looking as young and beautiful as she had when he'd first fallen in love with her, smiled right back.

And then, to his surprise, reached for him again.

TWELVE

"So that's what I did. When we got home, I admitted to Mamm and Daed that I'd disobeyed Harley, got stuck in a tree, and would've been alone in the woods if the Eight hadn't gotten me out. Just as I had expected, our father was mighty upset."

To Gabby's surprise, going to the Amish midwife with Kyle and his mother hadn't been as awkward or strange as she'd thought it was going to be. Milly was in her early thirties, very matter of fact and competent, and also incredibly comforting and kind. From the time Gabby first met her, to the private examination, to the later meeting with both Kyle and Mrs. Lambright, Gabby had felt at ease.

She'd also realized that she'd been guilty of harboring some pre-conceived prejudices that hadn't been fair at all. It seemed that even though she'd had many experiences to the contrary, her mother's views of Amish culture had rubbed off on her. She'd almost been expecting an old woman in a dark room ordering her about. Not the pleasant examining room in the back of Milly's house.

"How do you feel now?" Kyle

asked as they rode back to their house in the buggy. He was driving the horse and she was sitting snugly by his side. Mrs. Lambright was on Gabby's right. Sitting so close together felt a little awkward. But yet again, Mrs. Lambright's sweet demeanor and Kyle's positive manner made the journey easier than she'd anticipated.

"I feel a lot less nervous," Gabby admitted. "I wasn't sure what to expect would happen at an Amish midwife."

"Did you think she would be a lot different than a regular *doktah*?"

"Yes." Feeling self-conscious, she added, "No offense, Emma."

Kyle's mother chuckled softly. "None taken. You forget that I spent a lot of time with all of my *kinner*'s friends. Most were Amish, but many were not. Because of that, I'm used to giving most people the benefit of the doubt."

"I guess that's worked in my benefit."

Emma's eyes widened. "Not at all, Gabby. Kyle's father and I have liked you from the moment we first met."

Taking a chance, Gabby glanced at Kyle, then said, "I'm sure you wish Kyle had dated another girl . . ."

"You two will be fine, Gabby. The Lord makes His plans, *jah*? I wish you wouldn't worry so."

"I'll try not to," she promised, but she knew that would be a hard promise to keep. Everything in her life was so different right now, and her future was so up in the air. She wasn't sure what was going to happen.

"Well, look at that. I didn't expect to see him here," Kyle said as he slowed the buggy near the barn.

Gabby turned to look where Kyle was staring and felt a jolt of surprise. Lane was sitting on the Lambright's front porch steps and watching them pull up.

"Who is that?" Emma asked.

"Gabby's brother." Kyle didn't sound pleased. "Gabby, what do you want me to do? Do you want to see him, or should I ask him to leave?"

She'd been so shocked to see her

brother that it took Gabby a long minute to reply.

"I can't believe Lane is here," she whispered. "What do you think he wants?" Though he hadn't been mean to her before she left, he hadn't stopped by. Not one time. She'd been disappointed but had figured that her mother had convinced him to stay away.

But maybe that hadn't been the case at all?

Kyle set the brake on the buggy. "Let's go see."

Though a part of her wanted to avoid him, she nodded. She'd already learned that avoiding uncomfortable topics didn't necessarily make them go away.

"One thing at a time, Gabby," his

mother said as she slid down from the buggy. "Remember?"

"I remember. Thank you," Gabby said as Kyle helped her down.

Feeling Kyle's strong hands on her waist, she exhaled. No matter what happened, she had Kyle, and that was most important. Besides, Emma was right. All worrying about the worst possible scenario would ever do for her was make her even more stressed-out.

"We'll be all right, Mamm," Kyle murmured.

Emma smiled. "I think that is true. I'll be just inside if you two need me."

"*Jah,* Mamm. *Danke.*" Smiling at Gabby again before looking at Lane, he said, "Let me go put

Lightning back in his stall."

She nodded but didn't walk over to the house until Kyle returned to her side.

As they walked over, Lane watched them silently.

Gabby didn't think he looked angry, just tense. When they got near, he at last stood up.

"Hey," he said.

"Lane," Kyle said with a nod.

"Hi," she said simply. "I didn't expect to see you here."

He hung his head before lifting his chin and speaking. "I should've come over the day you moved out. Or in the weeks since."

Yes, he should have.

All their lives she'd tried to make things easier for him. But now all she wanted to do was make him see that she might be his older sister but that she had feelings, too. "Why didn't you?"

"You know why. Mom."

He was actually going to blame his actions on their mother? Gabby was sure she hadn't been around. He was also sixteen. He wasn't a small child, he could have found a way to come over to the Lambrights' home if he'd really wanted to.

"Okay," she said at last. "I guess that tells me everything I need to know." And yes, she had let a good dose of sarcasm seep into her tone.

Kyle edged closer to her, offering her support. "Let's go inside. Gabby could probably use a glass of water, and you could, too."

"Thanks, but I can't," Lane said. "I need to get to class. I really just wanted to tell you that I'm sorry that I worried so much about Mom that I wasn't around for you. But that's changed. I want to be here for you . . . and the baby."

She scanned his face, noticing that he looked as sincere as his words sounded. "Does Mom know you came over here?" she asked quietly.

His chin lifted. "Yes."

Hope flared. "Did she encourage you to stop by?" Maybe things with her mom were going to get better after all.

He shook his head. "Nah. I told her I wanted to see you, that there was no way I was going to kick you out of my life, even if she did."

"What did she say to that?"

"Not a lot, but she didn't yell or anything." He shrugged. "Can I stop over later this week? Will you be around?"

"Yeah. I'll be around." She looked at Kyle.

Once again, he didn't disappoint. "Anytime you want to come over to see Gabby, just show up, Lane," he said. "No matter what."

"Thanks," Lane said before pulling Gabby into a quick, awkward hug.

She hugged him back before he dropped his arms and hurried to his car — her old Camry.

As they watched him leave, Kyle

said, "Does it bother you that he is driving your car now?"

She thought about her answer before speaking. "No. He needs it more than me." And that really was the truth. She had moved on.

"You sound so sure about that."

"I am. See, I have you now." Gabby smiled up at him.

The smile he returned meant the world to her. And so did the sweet kiss and hug he gave her, too.

"Let's go inside and get you something to eat before I go help my brother," he said as he started walking.

His words reassured her that everything, no matter how new or stressful it might be, was going to be just fine.

THIRTEEN

"But I hadn't expected Harley to stay by my side when I told my story."

Another week had passed. After taking a leave of absence from her job, Gabby settled into the Lambrights' routine. On some days, she'd even felt like part of the family. She'd stopped being so worried about doing or saying the wrong things. Instead, she'd just decided to do her best, knowing that was enough for Kyle and his family.

Actually, she'd gotten so relaxed that she hadn't really been watching what she'd been doing when she'd tripped over a forgotten hoe and fell hard on the cement.

Mr. Lambright had been the one to rush to her side. "Gabby? Gabby, are you all right, child?"

She struggled to sit up. "I think so." Though tears were in her eyes, she attempted to shake them off. "That hoe got the best of me. I guess I should've been looking where I was going."

"Someone should have cleaned up after themselves." He stood and helped her to her feet. When he noticed her wince, he frowned. "We better take you to the hospital, I think."

All she could think about was the expense and the trouble. "No, I'm fine. It was just a silly mistake."

"Perhaps. But silly mistakes can have serious consequences, *jah*?" Before she could say another word, he murmured, "It's better to be safe than sorry," before telling her to sit down while he walked down the street to the phone shanty that they shared with a couple of other families and called for a driver.

Now, sitting in the hospital bed and hooked up to a monitor, Gabby kept repeating William's words of wisdom to herself. Tripping over a forgotten hoe and falling hard on the cement had been a stupid accident, but it really was better to be safe than sorry. She realized that even though she'd been upset about the baby initially, he or she was very much wanted now. She needed to take special care.

At first Gabby had been surprised that William hadn't insisted on them going to see Milly, the midwife. But he'd shaken his head and said that in this instance they should take advantage of modern technology.

As the monitor beeped and the blood pressure cuff tightened on her arm, Gabby shifted uncomfortably. Though the room was relatively quiet and everyone had been very nice, she was still surprised at how uneasy she felt in the sterile environment.

During the six weeks that she'd lived with the Lambright family, she had gradually become accustomed to a warmer, more familiar environment. The rushing nurses, brusque doctors, and cold cotton sheets on her hospital bed were a far cry from Kyle's family and the soft, worn sheets, blankets, and quilts that she now slept on.

"Gabby?"

Startled, she turned to the open doorway. After checking her in and sitting by her side when the nurses took her vitals, William had vacated the room. She knew he was giving her privacy, as well as attempting to reach the rest of the family.

He'd obviously been successful, because there was Kyle. He was still dressed in his work clothes, and his shirt looked a little damp from sweat. But his face and hair looked damp and freshly scrubbed.

He also looked panicked.

"Hey," she said. "I'm okay."

He crossed the room and reached for her hand. "Are you sure? You've got a lot of machines hooked up to you."

"I know, but they don't hurt or anything."

Still looking stricken, he said, "I'm so sorry I wasn't at home with you."

"You were working at Emerson's remodel with Harley. That was important. I was fine with your dad."

"And I *canna* believe you tripped

over a hoe. I'll see who left it out and —"

"You'll do no such thing. It was simply an accident."

He didn't look like he believed her. "An accident that could have been prevented." Looking increasingly pained, he murmured, "I'll never forgive myself if something happens to our babe."

"The doctor already listened for the heartbeat and did a sonogram. He said it's okay. He just wants me to stay here for a couple more hours to be on the safe side."

"They're sure that everything's all right?"

"They're as sure as anyone can be, I think." She squeezed his fingers. "Calm down. You're going to make me stressed-out, staring at me like that."

He exhaled. "Sorry." After kissing her knuckles, he moved to sit on the side of her bed. "I *canna* tell you how glad I am to see you looking so good. My heart nearly stopped when Harley told me the news."

"Harley told you?"

"*Jah. Mei daed* called Harley from the shanty, and then Harley told me. I couldn't get over here fast enough."

Warmth spread through her as his sweet words sank in. This was the type of man Kyle was — the type to drop everything to be by her side.

"I'm not going to lie, I was pretty

scared there for a while, too," she admitted. "But your *daed* really helped. He was the one who said we needed to call for a driver and get to the hospital."

He grinned. "There is something between you and Daed that's mighty special. I'm glad, but it never fails to take me by surprise."

Thinking about how well she got along with Kyle's rather formidable, rarely smiling father, she smiled back at him. "Sometimes I feel the same way."

It was then that he noticed the bandages on her palm and her knee and cheek. "Gabby, you are hurt."

"Just a few cuts and scrapes from when I fell. I think I was trying to make sure I didn't land on my belly."

"When we get you home, I'll sit with you on the couch and you can take a nap."

"That sounds perfect." She couldn't wait to get home, which was now a beautiful old Amish house.

Rubbing her knuckles with a thumb, Kyle cleared his throat. "Ahh, Gabby, this is probably the worst timing in the world, but I want, no, I need you to know that what we have between us isn't just for now. I want us to be a family."

Though they'd talked about their love for each other, neither of them had spoken too much about their future.

They'd done that at the encouragement of his parents. After sharing that they hoped that she and Kyle would always be a couple, his parents had also cautioned that both parenthood and marriage were for a lifetime. Mr. and Mrs. Lambright had even said that they'd thought it was possible for her and Kyle to be good parents even if they had to wait to enter into a relationship that they weren't ready for.

"We will be a family, no matter what happens to you and me," she said lightly.

He leaned closer. Pressed a light kiss to her brow. "*Nee,* that isn't what I mean." Drawing in a breath, he said, "Gabby, I want you to be my wife."

She gaped at him. Had he really just said what she thought he'd said?

"I'm trying to tell you that I already think I love our baby, but I *know* I love you and I want you forever. Will you marry me?"

A lump had formed in her throat and her eyes were stinging. She inhaled sharply, trying to retain her composure. "Kyle —"

He cut her off. "*Nee,* listen. I promise to work hard. We won't always have to live with my parents and siblings either. One day, we'll get a home of our own."

Though they hadn't talked much about their future, they had talked about how she wasn't ready to become Amish. As much as she loved living with the Lambrights, she'd learned that converting to the Amish faith meant more than being willing to ride around in a buggy or make do without electricity. It was an adoption of a whole way of life and adherence to faith that she wasn't ready for.

Which meant that Kyle was the one who was going to have to change.

"Kyle . . . are you certain about not being Amish?"

"*Jah.*"

"Really?"

He laughed. "Yeah." He winked. "Does that sound English enough for you?"

She smiled happily. "It does, but I don't need you to sound English.

Just to be certain."

"I am. I really am."

"Then I am, too. I'm certain about being your wife, Kyle."

"So, is that a yes?"

"It is." Raising her face to his, she murmured, "I'm so happy."

"Me, too." Just as he leaned down to kiss her, his father walked in.

He stood at the doorway and grunted. "Ah, here you are, son. Kissing Gabby yet again."

"We've got a good reason, Daed," Kyle said. "I just asked Gabby to be my wife and she said yes."

Gabby looked over at William and smiled. "It looks like you're stuck with me forever, Will . . ." Her voice drifted off as she saw who was standing right behind Kyle's father.

"Mom?"

Her mother, looking shaken and maybe even a little scared, said, "Gabrielle, I know you're surprised to see me, but I couldn't stay away. Not any longer."

Staring at her, then at Kyle and William, Gabby wondered what, exactly, her mother meant.

FOURTEEN

"Late that night, I knocked on Harley's door and asked him why he'd stayed with me."

Kyle knew he was wearing what Gabby teasingly called his "Amish face." It actually wasn't anything Amish, but rather something very "Lambright." It was his father's usual resting expression, where all his features were so set that no emotion seeped through.

As he stood next to Gabby's hospital bed, feeling tension radiating from Gabby — and fighting his own confusing thoughts — Kyle couldn't help it, though.

So many things had just happened, he could hardly keep up. And he was feeling so many warring emotions, it was a wonder his head wasn't about to explode.

He was grateful that Gabby hadn't gotten seriously hurt during her fall. Elated that she'd just said yes to his proposal. He was also confused and, yes, angry that her mother had shown up right at that moment. Especially when she'd been nothing but silent for weeks.

Therefore, he was coping by tamping everything down. Kyle didn't know if that was the "right" way to act, or if there even was a "right" way to be. All he did know was that his only concern at the moment was for Gabby.

He moved closer to her, watching her expression carefully. He knew right then and there that if her mother made her cry, he would shuttle her out the door immediately.

Her mother was still standing awkwardly in the doorway. Half in, half out. Every other time he'd seen her, she'd been dressed stylishly, wearing a lot of makeup, and her hair had been down upon her shoulders.

Today? She had her hair in a limp ponytail, was wearing a faded pair of jeans, tennis shoes, and a sweatshirt, and hardly any paint on her face. He actually thought she looked younger and far more approachable.

Or maybe it had more to do with the way Karen Ferrara was looking at Gabby. There was doubt and longing in her eyes, and a foreign tentativeness that Kyle had never expected to see.

And because of that, some of the coldness he felt for her thawed a bit.

He glanced at his father. He was remaining silent, but he was staring at him intently. Kyle knew his *daed* was waiting for him to do the right thing.

But what was that?

Kyle knew he wasn't prepared to do anything other than what Gabby wanted.

Turning to her, he reached for Gabby's hand again and examined her face. She looked confused but not upset.

"Mom, what are you doing here?" Gabby said after another second or two passed.

"Well, um . . . William here called and talked some sense in me."

"My father called you?" Kyle blurted. Just then, he noticed his mother had joined them. She was standing in the middle of the hallway. He reckoned his *mamm* was doing her best to stay out of the way but was eager to jump in to help.

"I did," Daed said. "I figured Karen would want to know about

Gabby's fall." Smiling at Gabby, he added, "I thought it also might be time to try to smooth things out. Ain't so?"

Gabby smiled softly at Kyle's father. "Yes."

That interplay seemed to be the encouragement Gabby's mom needed. Stepping into the room at last, she said, "I think I was being foolish and stubborn. I had been so hurt by Paul, it was difficult for me to remember that all Amish men aren't alike."

Gabby clutched Kyle's arm. "Paul?"

"Yes. That is your father's name, Gabrielle. His name is Paul Yoder."

Gabby looked up at Kyle. He shrugged. He'd never heard of the man, but he wasn't too surprised. There were a lot of Amish in the area. His parents entered the hospital room just in time to hear the tail end of Karen's words. Looking up at them, he said, "Mamm? Daed? Do you know this man?"

His father shook his head. "*Nee*. I don't know a Paul Yoder. Does he still live in the community?"

Karen shook her head. "He lives in Indiana now." After taking a sigh, she added, "Gabby, I want you to know that part of the reason that I've been staying away is because I was trying to locate him and tell him about you and the baby."

Gabby's eyes were wide. "But, Mom, you hate him."

"Well, *hate* might have been a strong word, but you're right. I can't deny that I have no good feelings for that man. But I realized that I had to do the right thing for you."

"Did you find him?" Gabby asked.

Karen nodded. "It took me a while, but I actually did. He works for a furniture company out in Shipshewana."

Gabby looked like she was about to cry.

After glancing at his parents' stunned expressions, Kyle perched on the side of Gabby's bed and wrapped an arm around her shoulders. When she leaned toward him, he rubbed her back a few times then said, "What did this Paul say?"

Karen's expression became almost as harsh as his father's "Amish face." "Paul told me that he'd married and that his wife, children, and extended family had no idea about me or Gabby and he intended for it to stay that way." She swallowed.

"What a snake!" his *mamm* said.

Smiling grimly, Karen nodded. "Then he had the nerve to offer to send Gabby some money."

"I hope you told him what he could do with it," Gabby muttered.

Karen's eyes lit up. "I sure did. I gave him my address and told him to send it right away."

Kyle covered his mouth in a poor attempt to cover his shock.

Gabby, on the other hand, looked completely incredulous. "Mom, did you really do that? Why?"

"Because you deserve it."

Gabby shook her head. "No."

Karen's voice softened. "Gabrielle, I've loved being your mother. I've never regretted my decision to have you and raise you by myself. But it was hard. There were many, many months I thought I might not be able to pay rent, or our bills, or make sure you had enough warm clothes. Of course, things got better for a while after I met and married Lane's dad, but you went without a lot."

She pulled out an envelope from her purse. "I received the money yesterday. It's yours."

Gabby shook her head again. "I don't want it."

"I thought you might say that, which is why I'm glad Kyle and his parents are here with you." Looking at Kyle directly, she said, "I hope you'll hold on to this for Gabby."

"Nee," he replied. "If Gabby doesn't want it, then I don't either."

"I know all about pride, Kyle. It's what kept me from ever forcing Paul to accept me or our daughter. It hurt too much to ever see myself from his point of view — as his mistake." She lifted her chin. "But I have to say that I did learn something along the way, and that's that while pride might fuel your insides, it doesn't feed your children."

She glanced at his parents before speaking again. "Look, Gabby, I know your situation is completely different from mine. You'll never be alone like I was. You have Kyle and his parents and me and Lane. None of us will ever allow you to feel like you have no one to rely on. But now you have an extra security blanket, too."

Kyle glanced at his parents, who were now looking at Karen with a lot more respect. His mother darted a glance his way and slowly nodded.

He turned to Gabby, who still was clutching his hand in a death grip. "Gabrielle, I have to say she has a point."

"Mom, I never thought about

what you had to go through. I mean, I guess I did, but I never really thought about what it must have been like." Her voice lowered. "It must have been so hard."

Her mother shrugged. "That doesn't matter now. Like I said, I've made my own mistakes. Please take it, Gabby. Paul is going to regret his choice to never know you, I'm sure of that. But we might as well let him do this. It's not enough, but it's more than I ever expected."

"All right," Gabby said.

Kyle leaned forward and took the envelope from Gabby's mother. He knew that not only was she trying to make amends, but she was also trying to make a difference for her grandchild's life. He could appreciate that.

His action seemed to push Gabby out of her stupor. "Are you sure, Mom? I didn't pay any of the bills. Maybe you should keep some of it."

"Absolutely not."

Kyle's mother spoke. "I think it's time we all sat down, don't you? I could ask the nurse to bring us more chairs."

Looking uncomfortable again, Karen shook her head. "Now that I know you are okay, I think I'll go ahead and leave and let Gabby rest. But, Gabby, when you are ready, maybe you could give me a call and I could stop by soon?"

"I'd like that, Mom."

"Me, too." Her mother smiled. "I really am so sorry about how I reacted when you told me your news. I should've been better."

Gabby nodded. "I love you, Mom, but I want you to know that it's going to take me some time to get over it. I mean, if not for Kyle, I would've been on the street. I would have had nowhere to go."

"I know. And I don't expect you to forgive me easily. Maybe I don't even expect Kyle to ever forgive me. What I did was awful and inexcusable. But I can only say that what I did was a knee-jerk reaction. I wanted to apologize almost right away, but I didn't know how. I am very sorry."

Kyle pressed his lips to Gabby's brow. "What do you think?" he whispered.

"I don't know."

Kyle leaned close and whispered into her ear again. "Life isn't fair, but it doesn't mean that you can't forgive her."

She inhaled, looking ready to disagree, when a new sense of peace seemed to envelop her. Then, she nodded.

Kyle relaxed. Gabby understood what he'd meant. Forgiveness didn't need to be a mutual or a reasonable decision after hours of worry. No, all that was needed was a steadfast heart.

Looking over at her mom, Gabby said softly, "I forgive you, Mom."

Karen had tears in her eyes now. "Thank you. I promise, I'll try to make it up to you."

Pushing away the bitterness that she'd been holding close, Gabby recalled everything her mother had done for her. All of the sacrifices, the working long hours, the time she'd taken on extra clients in the evenings so that Gabby could take gymnastic lessons. No, she wasn't perfect, but Gabby knew she wasn't perfect, either. No one was.

"You don't need to make up anything, Mom. As long as you can learn to accept me and Kyle and the baby, there's nothing more you will ever need to do."

Her mother smiled tentatively at Kyle. "Already done."

When Kyle reached for Gabby's hand again, he knew everything was going to be better. At last.

Fifteen

" 'I stayed with you so you'd always remember that you're never alone, Kyle,' Harley had said in that quiet way of his. 'I wanted to make sure you knew that even when I'm mad at you, or when I don't agree with something you say or do, I'll never leave your side. Just like the Lord will never leave you.' He had looked at me intently, then said, 'One day, I hope you'll do the same for someone else.' "

Two Months Later

They'd weighed all the options but in the end decided that only a marriage sooner, rather than later, would do. Kyle had said it best — they might be young and have a lot of differences to get used to and make up for, but they had in abundance what mattered the most: love.

Gabby was very glad that they'd made the decision to have a quiet, family-only ceremony just two weeks ago. It hadn't been the wedding of her little girl dreams — there was no long white gown, no huge group of friends, or five bridesmaids dressed in matching gowns.

But she had worn a simple white

dress and carried a bouquet of pale pink roses that Kyle had brought her that morning.

The ceremony hadn't taken place in a beautiful old church. Instead, it had been in front of a justice of the peace and a pastor from the church that she and Kyle had recently begun attending. The vows had been the same, which turned out was all that had mattered.

And while they hadn't had a huge reception with piles of gifts, the dinner that Emma, Beth, and Betty had cooked had been wonderful. As had the company and the warm hugs.

But maybe the best part of it all — besides Kyle, of course — was the part Lane and her mother had played. Lane had walked her down the aisle and her mother had made a real wedding cake from scratch, and had even arranged Gabby's long hair into a beautiful updo that had been the hairstyle of her dreams.

Her mother's presence had been something she hadn't counted on but had been so grateful for. As had her gift to Gabby and Kyle — a wedding night in the honeymoon suite in a local hotel.

Things hadn't turned out like she'd dreamed, but she had a feeling that she was never going to regret one second of what had happened.

God had played a part in everything and had reminded all of them again and again just what was important.

"Gut matin, frau," Kyle called out as he came inside. "Wait, what are you doing up?"

"When I saw that you were already out of bed, I decided to get up, too." Finally, she noticed that he was holding a basket and a carafe from a nearby coffee shop. "Kyle, what's that?"

"A decaf mocha latte with chocolate croissants."

There was a time not too long ago when he would have had no idea what either of those things were — or where to get them.

"You went to The Coffee Shack?"

"I did."

He looked so pleased with himself. Like he was gloating. "Why? What did you get my favorite things for?"

"Because it's our two-week anniversary and I wanted to do something special for you."

Taking a bite out of the croissant, which was still warm, she almost moaned. "This is really special," she said. "Perfectly special. Thank you so much."

"It wasn't much."

For him to go out and take the time to get her things like this? It was everything. Just like everything he'd done. He'd loved her even though they were so different.

He'd accepted her pregnancy with a maturity some men twice his age might not have possessed.

He'd brought her to his house, persuaded his family to give her a place to live, and had stood by her side even when her own family hadn't.

And then, when Lane and her mother had come around, he'd gifted them with forgiveness and accepted them into his life.

Finally, he'd married her and had even elected not to become baptized in the Amish church, choosing to slowly make his own path by her side, as her husband.

"I wish I had something for you."

"You're here. That's enough, don't you think?"

"I don't know about that."

He sat down on the couch beside her. "Well, then how about this?

You are going to give me the most special gift of all, the most precious gift a person can receive, our baby."

At times like these, she felt like there weren't enough words in the dictionary to try to convey her feelings. But maybe that was the point.

Sometimes one's heart was so full that no words were necessary or needed.

Because he was right. God had given them the most wonderful gift of all. A future so bright and full of hope that few things could ever compare.

"Here," she said at last, holding out the croissant. "Come share my breakfast, Kyle."

He took a bite from her hand, wrapped an arm around her shoulders, and propped his feet on the ottoman next to hers.

Together, they sipped her mocha latte and ate chocolate pastries and watched the morning light break through the clouds on the horizon.

No, life wasn't perfect, but it was very, very good.

Precious, even.

A precious, beautiful gift.

ACKNOWLEDGMENTS

I never meant to write this story. It wasn't in my contract, it wasn't in my schedule, and I really didn't have time to write even a very short novella like *A Precious Gift*. But sometimes the characters in a book seem to take a life of their own. That's what happened with Gabby and Kyle!

Gabby and Kyle were secondary characters in *The Loyal One*. I only created their story line to add some depth to *The Loyal One*'s hero,

Harley Lambright. But by the time I finished the book, I felt like they had their own story to tell, too! First, I asked Lynne, my beta reader, what she thought. It turns out that she had already written on her notes to me that she wanted to know what happened to them ASAP. :)

That's when I asked Marla Daniels, my editor at the time, for a phone call. When we talked, I rambled on about my ideas and she listened very patiently. Then I asked if I could please write one more novella in the series. She did some thinking and some checking, and before I knew it, I was given permission to write *A Precious Gift.*

As things happen in publishing

houses, I was passed on to another editor, Molly Gregory, by the time I finished this story. So it's Molly who helped me fine-tune this story into something that actually made sense. Now I have Sara Quaranta, a third editor, who has been championing this story as it goes through final stages into publication.

I'm so grateful for the whole team at Gallery for taking the time to help bring *A Precious Gift* to life. No book of mine ever gets published without a great many people behind it, and this story is a good example of that.

So with that, I'd like to officially thank Marla, Molly, and Sara, three editors who made this author feel so very blessed.

ABOUT THE AUTHOR

A practicing Lutheran, **Shelley Shepard Gray** is the *New York Times* and *USA TODAY* bestselling author of more than eighty novels, translated into multiple languages. In her years of researching the Amish community, she depends on her Amish friends for gossip, advice, and cinnamon rolls. She lives in Colorado with her family and writes full time.